I0838137

A Memory of Fictions

(or)

Just Titty-Boom

By

LEONCE GAITER

LEGBA BOOKS

A Memory of Fictions

(or)

Just Tiddy-Boom

Published by Legba Books

ISBN: 979-8-9902899-0-1

www.LeonceGaiter.com

Printed in U.S.A.

"One school reasons that the present is undefined, that the future has no other reality than as present hope, that the past is no more than present memory. Another school declares that the whole of time has already happened and that our life is a vague memory or dim reflection, doubtless false and fragmented, of an irrevocable process."

— Jorge Luis Borges, "Tlon, Uqbar, Orbis, Tertius"

Chapter I

WHITE TRASH STOLE MY WHEEL

Los Angeles, 1986

Jessie woke to a tinny radio alarm screaming the morning news. He rose from the folding futon he had spread the night before, this in his one-room, ground-floor barrio apartment that despite extraordinary efforts still smelled of previous tenants' cigarettes, feet, and beer. Paint peeled off the walls—walls behind which innumerable generations of roaches had made their homes. On closer inspection, (and he inspected closely once he had sprayed with poisons to the point of his own asphyxiation), they had appendages no insect should. Mutants, probably. With his luck, probably a plague-carrying strain.

The next moment, mariachi music blasted through the window. The whole building shook to the beat of the oom-pah bass. A maudlin voice through accordion chords wailed about his *corazón*. He could have ripped the *corazón* from whoever was blaring that car radio at 7:30 am. He flashed on an image of himself striding outside in his shorts, thrusting his hand through the open car window, deep into that chest, and wrenching forth the heart—the shocked, bewildered faces of the neighbors wailing wildly in abject horror, blabbering madly in Spanish, crossing themselves furiously and convinced they had glimpsed the devil itself.

He steamed impotently until the car drove off, the thunderous bass trailing after it. In the sudden silence, he opened the window to let some air in.

"Puta!" WHAP! Through window he heard the palm smack her face and the wounded woman's cry. Looking out, Jessie saw the man turn and walk away, as she followed, her eyes red and tearing, both hands to the burning cheek.

He closed the window.

In the tiny hallway between the bathroom and the front door, he opened his small closet for the artful task of dressing. He chose the underpants with the fewest holes; ditto the socks. On the ground sat three old, well-worn pairs of shoes. Today, he chose the black topsiders, the soles of which were split, but such that no one could tell unless he crossed his legs in the masculine fashion—not likely. The clothes were mildly tattered but clean, well-matched, and tasteful. Since they hailed from his better days, their wornness could pass for chic dishevelment.

Once dressed, he loaded his slim wallet in his back pocket, took enough change to board the bus, with transfer, and headed for work.

Such were the depths to which Jessie Vincent Grandier III had sunk.

He had not been a fall down, gutter drunk, or one that wept on barstools at the mention of "mother" or "friendship." In public, he drank moderately and behaved well. It was in private, behind locked doors, that he punished himself like a vicious child who had trapped some writhing creature. He had never foreseen such a fall, had not been raised to think events so chipped-flint sharp could cut him, so bright and loud could blind and deafen him. His senses had been tuned to the American lie of ease and subtler things. Dulcet tones. Muted hues.

After graduating from Harvard, he had barely set foot in his father's house in the DC suburbs before he fled to Los Angeles where he soon took his first TV job—in the mailroom. He had never been west of the Mississippi and rarely far from the academic underbellies of New York and Boston. He had come to make his mark in film, to wring through great art a deliverance from the strange, vaudevillian, death-besotted saga of his life. He had studied film under pot-bellied semioticians and weasly philosophy PhD's, men who spoke of films in terms of sacred texts—a language in which Jessie had grown proudly fluent and knew—just knew—to be the standard lexicon of all film folk.

As with so much in his young life, the joke would be on him.

*****

On hearing of his plans to move to Los Angeles, Jessie's father suggested he live with one of his two

LA relations, Cousins Alma or Fred, but preferred he live with Alma, for she, as he put it, lived "right in the middle of everything" while Fred lived, "way the hell out there" in Beverly Hills.

Alma lived in the ghetto.

Jessie's plane hit LA at night. He sat in Alma's car on the ride from the airport leering out the windows at the moonlit noir-ness, the palm trees, the stucco, the gaudy, freeway-ribboned, incandescent sprawl. It was so much like he had pictured it. Gazing out those windows, Jessie imagined himself cinematically larger than life: on the lam, running, perhaps scared, definitely lethal.

The next day, he faced with shock the sun-blanched reality of the world beyond the Ivy—league, that is.

Jessie was not accustomed to poor people, nor black folks who did not conform to the New Orleans/ Creole college-educated striver mold. As an Army child, he had lived many places, at home and abroad, in most of them surrounded by white people. His mother avoided his father's family like the plague, and her people, among whom the children sometimes lived, came from Africans who, generations ago, interbred with the visiting Spanish and French such that skin honeyed, hair loosened, features remolded. Although black, individually and culturally they crowned themselves unique. Often monied, the cream of New Orleans' black coffee, the most outrageous of them, the ones from whom Jessie had sprung, bore themselves with a mixture of semi-courtly majesty and gutbucket sass that Jessie had come to think of as the universal black folk norm (just as he thought Hollywood filled to spillage with semioticians).

To open the door that morning, walk outside, hit main drag Crenshaw Boulevard, and hear consonant clusters drop like pennies and the non-ironic use of "ain't" . . . to be welcomed to the neighborhood by a young woman sporting a nametag reading, "Aquanetta," her striped uniform dotted with orange game birds identifying her as off-to-work preparing greasy chicken dishes . . . this shocked him. It would have been one thing if he could have dismissed them, like he would have hillbillies. But with them he shared a common ancestry. How, oh how, could similar cultural underpinnings have produced someone called "Aquanetta" and himself?

Jessie's cousin Fred, Alma's brother (and arch enemy because he was rich and lived in Beverly Hills and she wasn't and didn't) still worked the original fount of his current wealth, a veterinary office on the corner of a once middle-class black neighborhood, now gone to seed. His naugahyde lobby, unchanged since the '60s, smelled faintly of dog and if you traveled through the double doors, the smell overwhelmed you as you reached the tiny back apartment in which Jessie's Uncle Bernard lived. He was about seventy, and one of those old men who seemed outrageously fat, though he was not huge. The fat had just invaded every crack and crevice in him. His fingertips, his ankles, his knees. Some was swelling. Bernard drank, too.

Bernard drank like a blaring object lesson. He gave the impression he had really worked and yearned for something years ago, but you couldn't figure what. You couldn't separate the bluster, the bravado and lies, from the truth, but occasionally, something set him alight, and the heightened lucidity bespoke honesty. During Jessie's slow, relentless fall, the January 1943 Carnegie Hall Concert recording of the historic performance of Duke Ellington's uncut "Black Brown and Beige" was released on vinyl. Jessie couldn't afford it, but he bought it anyway. Now, guilty, he visited Bernard to borrow money. Sixty dollars. Not much. He wanted and needed more but wouldn't get it since poor Bernard was the only one from whom he wasn't too embarrassed to borrow. At the veterinary office, they sent him to a bar down the street called the Ten Spot.

Fifties style red-shaded lamps hung down above the tables—cool lighting, dim but not sleazy, reeking of jukebox Dinah Washington and troubles you tell no one. Semi-circular booths, the kind in which, drink in hand, you forge friendships through raucous laughter, the point of which you may forget, but the memory of which you keep forever. The faces leaned over the bar, full of lines and forgetting, and all of this looked like it might have looked years and years ago. Jessie had dreamt places like this. He dreamt himself in them, full of his own imaginary black people, the ones he loved, who, unlike the white ones, accepted their dying, sometimes piss poorly but they accepted it, who ate bitterness and want, who digested it and made it part of themselves, knew rage, against white men and God, and could still wake each day and do what they had to, who didn't confuse themselves with God, and, sick with power, make everything in heaven and earth smaller than they were, and then, contemptuous, kill or demean it.

Bernard sat there, alone at a booth. The afternoon sun streamed in through the stained glass windows, shifting the deep reds of the place to burnished orange, and his face merged with the sun and woods and red-globed lanterns, with the emptiness and the slow song, the voice tired, resigned, and almost amused, that played on the box. His eyes were too large, bloodshot, and his hair speckled with a dirtying gray. His brown skin was still smooth, though, the damage he inflicted showing mainly in airs, and girth, and in the worn, tired eyes.

"Wish I could do moh fo' ya'," he said in a voice weak from liquor and cigarettes, not even gravelly, or raspy or any of those things that might have lent it distinction. "But I'm not one o' the money folks. I'm poh folk." He laughed, tongue inching through the lips, a tortured sound like an asthmatic urgently blowing a balloon. They talked of the music for a while, Jessie mentioning the Ellington album. He couldn't confess to buying it, not while he sat here bumming sixty bucks for food to eat.

"I knew her back in the ole days," Bernard said when Jessie mentioned the girl singer, Betty Roche. "Back in Nyarlens." He said he jammed with her and other famous names, way back when. He talked of others he knew, musicians, most of them dead now, a few familiar names, but most players no one remembered except others like himself who heard them and knew their worth firsthand.

Jessie tried to imagine this old man young. Staring at that face he tried to whittle away the years from the eyes, whittle away the fat and the wear and tear to find a seed that could stand for the younger man. Since he could not, he rested on cliché: dark places like this one full of smart mouthed women in butt-tight cocktail dresses, the smell of hair tonic about them, tottering on heels after a few too many, their conked escorts full of swagger and bullshit. Colored folks, all of whom knew what a saxophone meant, and what Mahalia Jackson sounded like. His head said there was nothing to envy. Each generation, armed with the ray guns of romance, envies its predecessors. There was nothing in it. No truth to the rumor that black folks had lived on the other sides of mountains.

*

Having dressed in his worn best, Jessie crept from his barrio apartment, the socialist snoring mightily behind the bedroom door. He paced contentedly to the busstop that morning. It was lovely out, yesterday's rain having cleared the smog away. Even this dirty neighborhood looked welcoming. Across the street, tenement dwellers loaded their piecework from their sewing machine-filled apartments into a van. Mildly to severely overweight women dragged children to schools and busstops, little child voices like razors. Yuppies in Volvos and near-yuppies in Jeeps swept down this two-lane street, shortcutting to their jobs downtown, the towers of which were visible between the ramshackle apartment buildings. As he stood at the crosswalk, a streetsweeper roared past outpacing many a passenger car, occasionally swiping the piles of fast food wrappers, beer cans and Old Night Train bottles amassed in the gutters. The driver actually blared his horn at the slower cars in his path.

Jessie wondered if that dead thing was still there, the decomposition of which now fascinated him. It had shocked him at first. He'd assumed it was a cat. Then on closer inspection, he realized it was some wild thing, a possum maybe. That first day, he passed it with a subdued "eeuugghhh" and walked on. He assumed that some government bureau in charge of dead things would discard the corpse. He had forgotten where he was, a denizen of just *where* he had become. For the next two weeks that same rotting possum lay festering, a feast for ants and roaches, probably local cats and dogs accustomed to meals of rotting flesh. As the days passed, it began to look as if it had deflated. As if the life, along with the flesh, had just been . . . let out. There was something wrong when his world and that of wild, rotting creatures were not distinct. Some breaking point had been reached. Accommodation would have to be made.

On arriving at the bus stop, he stood with his nose pressed against the nearest wall, as if suddenly overwhelmed with grief or examining it for structural faults. This prevented positive identification by passing motorists. How humiliating to take the bus in LA. It meant carlessness, and in a town where fry cooks with shoes still damp from crossing the Rio Grande drove, carlessness bespoke a demeaning sort of poverty, the kind where you couldn't even scare up a few hundred for a passable wreck, and hadn't the resources, connections, or cool to turn over some quick drugs for the money.

The downslide, the slow, inexorable decline of Jessie Grandier had begun with the car, as so much does in LA. A few months out of St. Mary's Drug Rehabilitation Center in Minneapolis, Minnesota, he still lived in fashionable Beverly Hills Adjacent although he had been laid off from the low-level network TV executive job to which he had quickly climbed. Jessie owed two months' rent.

That building sat just off the Sunset Strip, an historic main drag dotted with rock 'n' roll clubs. The clubs sat nearly dark through the late '70s and early '80s, but now experiencing a renaissance through Heavy Metal. Skinny boys in skin-tight leather pants, long blond hair layered and dyed, studded bracelets about the wrists, and their girls in hooker/whore drag, tight mini-skirts and fishnets, tits bouncing (if they had them yet), and tripping in spike heels over any wound in the pavement. At closing time they spewed from the clubs, drunk and stumbling, yelling, fighting, fucking.

One presentimental night, Jessie came home to find a strange car jacked-up near his parking space. A gaunt, scruffy looking man, and a fat, dyed-blonde woman in skin-tight clothes and too much makeup hung out of the open doors of their tattered VW. Cigarettes dangled from their lips. He eyed them suspiciously. He went straight to his balcony to spy on them, but from that angle, he couldn't see anything. He should have confronted them, threatened them, called the police, done something. But he didn't. Cops unnerved him. He had a kitchen drawer full of unpaid bills. He had mistakenly opened it the previous week and immediately slammed it shut with a shudder. The registration had expired and the car was not insured. He waited. Eventually he fell asleep.

Next morning he found his little dented orange Datsun listing badly to one side. A wheel was gone. Not just flat, but gone. He could have screamed. In fact he did. A loud, low growl of woeful insult, for he knew this was the beginning of the end, the first stomach churning lurch on a long, steep, downhill plunge the end of which was nowhere near and the depths of which he couldn't imagine.

"White trash!" he spat, the outrage and portentousness palpable . . . *"White trash* stole my wheel!"

DATELINE LOS ANGELES—1988

An unquestionably ignorant, possibly senile ex-actor, having assumed the Presidency of the United States through ingeniously manipulating romantic iconography, outdated yet still potent, of great frontier boom lands begging settlement by lean and hearty white folks, in fact served as shield for corporate interests and wealthy individuals, reducing or eliminating restrictions on their financial behavior.

The country embarked on an unprecedented peacetime military buildup, with a reciprocal dwindling of non-military resources. Thus, many fell homeless, funds for safety-net programs for mental health and public housing slashed, they begged coins, dirty, sometimes dangerous, sleeping in paper on doorsteps, squatting in abandoned buildings, defecating on sidewalks, standing near freeways holding signs saying "will work for food." The number of Americans without health insurance rose dramatically, as did the cost of medical care. Hospitals turned away those without coverage. The infant mortality rate rose to the highest in the industrialized world. Funds for education dwindled across the fifty states. Inner cities, populated by blacks, Latinos, and other minorities were the hardest hit, commerce having abandoned their neighborhoods. The manufacturing base of the U.S. disappeared through government policies aligned with corporate greed to drive manufacturing to cheap third world labor sources to which U.S. corporations flocked. The inner city high school dropout rates shot to near fifty percent. Youth gang violence exploded and random drive-by shootings became a way of life.

It was America. You got by, that's all. You did what you had to, prayed for a windfall, bought that lottery ticket, hoped and prayed another chance might find you.

You got by.

Chapter II

GOD'S TROMBONES

When some billionaire succumbed to financial fashion and bought the TV network for which Jessie worked, layoff rumors flew. Soon, efficiency experts roamed the halls in gray suits and barbershop hairdos, sparking nervous whispers. Jessie and the other script readers in the Story Department thought themselves safe. How could a TV drama department survive without its editorial component? Someone had to read and "fix" the script of any proposed TV pilot. Plus, informal discussions with higher ups assured them, "You're fine." After the news . . . "We're sorry, but we'll be restructuring and . . ." He and his colleagues walked away from between five and fifteen years of their lives, not that surprised, but each feeling low, and ill-used.

"Just as well," Jessie thought, in a rare trip to the bright side, "something to get me off my ass and pointed in the right direction."

And he knew what that was. He had studied; he had mastered. Now he would *do*. He had known as far back as he remembered. In college, the specifics changed. Writing to film. That's all. There was still time.

He could still assume his birthright. He would wear that barbed wire mantle that hung in the back of his own mental closet like the family's long-lost crown. He would grin while the spikes drew his blood.

He had long detested self-aggrandizing portraits of young *Artistes,* sensitive, soulful wimps who got tripped up in school hallways and pined after big-breasted girls who didn't know their names. He resented their announcements that they walked the path to greatness. Some things should be secrets. To declare oneself, to tell them all, that was treason. It was as if he carried a cipher inside himself, which God had whispered, (Do you hear me!? GOD. No one less) in strictest confidence. That he would make beauty from nothing. That he would be more than a mere man.

He told no one. He feared such thoughts. How many foolishly believed they bore such predestined weight? If his notions were true, well then, he surely must be blessed, as few have been. He would know, perhaps on his deathbed, that that had been the case.

If they proved false . . . well, then, he cursed himself and his past, those god-damned liars, those vicious whisperers, for doing their job so well because he knew that these notions would not fade, no matter how he tried to best them. They would not fade. Not while he drew breath.

Double-cursed he was. Not born fool enough to let his own lies be. Laden with missives from God that might be fake.

She had already borne Janice and Talia, but his

father needed a boy. His father, the youngest of thirteen children, among them many males, not one having borne a son. The odds against this seemed extraordinary, clearly the work of impish, giggling gods. Jessie's father would thwart them, though, and produce an heir to the legacy of the Grandiers—a couple of acres of bayou swamp land and an uninhabitable hut—all prized by his family as if the last remnants of an empire.

Lulene embarked on a third pregnancy, despite doctors' warnings. They wanted to give her a hysterectomy after the second, but she refused. She had too much to gain by trying once more, by possessing what her husband so needed. She risked a lot, her life, at the hands of military doctors, Grandier (she always called him that—just "Grandier") being in the Army. Butchers with stethoscopes the lot. The black ones had an excuse, she thought. They joined up for medical degrees, the only way they could get them. But the white ones . . .

She had two girls they struggled to support. Janice, almost six by now, already covered her ears at night so not to hear the screams and beatings, blocking out words like "money" and "liquor" and "women," already accepting the role of strong and impervious child who soothed and solaced the mother. Talia had already conceived her self-involved cocoon, building it clandestinely, on the childish sly, like nighttime masturbation, thread by stolen thread, in which she would soon live unchallenged, and later emerge, she knew, even more beautiful. It was not right to bring another one into this for spite. Oh, but she would love him all the more for it. Even now she loved him all the more. "Him," she thought, because she knew. She took him to her bed, and there they stayed for months until his birth.

Creole women did things. Jessie once thought them cruel, but these women were more overt, less . . . sentimental, that's all. They never relinquished the winning cards from down their fronts. They always kept one bullet in the barrel. Her husband wanted a son like a junky the needle. She saw to it that there would be one forever just beyond his reach.

Lulene bore him, and her family of women set about anointing him. For them, Lulene did him up like a little Dauphin. Shorts suits, bow ties, white socks, and a pressed white shirt, wavy black hair slicked down and to the side. He'd take her hand, waist high to her, waist high to everyone, wide-eyed, shy, always proper, speaking when spoken to and speaking well, always aware that he was *of* her, an extension, looking like her, as if she had opened her mouth unnaturally wide and forced him out in some perversion of birth then cleaned up the spit and blood so no one would know what she'd done.

In a yacht-sized white Mercury with green trim around the fins, they traveled for what seemed like hours. They hit the edge of town, where train tracks met abandoned lots overgrown with huge thistly bushes. Trees clutched high white fences as if frightened. The sun beat down harder here—he had to squint to see—

and the clouds hung lower, as if you could reach up and pull them down to play with. Silent in the car, he fidgeted and squirmed. He counted to himself the churches they passed. He studied her face. He tried to see her eyes behind her dark glasses. He tried to read the expression on the expressionless lips, so wet and lush they might have dripped huge dollops of their red.

Ethel's compound stood behind a wall of trees and bushes. The car pulled up outside and sent a dust cloud floating up. Lulene climbed out, some near oriental-looking high-necked dress, silken black hair. Her copper colored skin seemed to change hue with every move as if playing its own gleeful game of tag with the sun. Jessie scrambled hurriedly from the car, crawling halfway across the expansive front seat to leap the chasm between the baseboard and the ground, knowing that for her every step he needed two to keep up. He grabbed her skirt and followed.

Aunt (pronounced "Ont" not "Ant," thank you) Ethel, Miss Honey, Missy. They were old by the time Jessie knew them, but age hadn't dulled them. Lulene's Aunt Ethel piled the pancake on pretty heavy, but the furs still shimmered and the diamonds like sparkling shackles still clamped her wrists. The fur cap tilted randily on her head, she was always off to one of her "balls" where other honey-colored people dripped fur and glimmered and shone. She looked every inch the dowager.

They walked through a vine-choked archway. A narrow path bordered a two-story apartment building in which Missy and Honey shared a home. Butch old lesbians who hunted and fished and brought back mounds of lobster and crab the women took to the kitchen and spent all day cleaning and cooking. Lulene's Aunt Missy had been beautiful, her hair, which fell to her knees, legendary.

At the back of the courtyard, beyond the swingset and the azalea-covered latticework sat Ethel's house. As the heavy oak door swung open, the smell of old things nearly knocked him down. Everything was huge inside. Sofas tensed on claws like lions in wait for prey. Bureaus sat brooding like Buddhas. Old pictures lined the wall outside the kitchen. Sepia-toned and cracked, there seemed to be hundreds of them, floor to ceiling. There were pictures of Lulene and her sister Shanice, born of different fathers, Lulene's a phantom Filipino who knocked up her mother and was dismissed; Shanice's some handsome black man sent packing for reasons no one bothered to remember. Lulene as a child, sitting on a pony, looking studied and proud even then, as Shanice looked on, plump, pretty, resenting Lulene's light skin and silky hair and preparing not to forgive the younger girl for blessings of beauty on top of those smaller gifts. Pictures showed Ethel draped in furs in '38, in clubs, with men, always men hovering about, drinks in hand, hair conked, mustaches trimmed; pretty women in cocktail dresses, walking on clouds of sound from horns so lush and rich you could have laid down on them and slept, Ellington, God's Trombones. They wore men like garments, perused them like sale items. A man's loving was a virtue. Some offered that. Others paid for company. They married some, and slept with, sometimes loved, others. Ethel had a house full of what, with her, became antiques, gifts from men she married and left, or loved and outlived.

They danced at the top of the hill, these women and their men, unfettered by whites and their earthbound ways. Their shops, their streets, and their customs defined their own complete and melismatic world. They knew white folks hadn't a clue. Gingham and pewter. Whites knew nothing of silk. They might buy it, but they couldn't live it. Sure, when Ethel and Missy drove any distance they'd spend all day cooking, knowing they couldn't eat at white joints on the way. They'd travel in clothes to sleep in, knowing they'd rest in the car. They wanted their own, these people . . . their own hotels, and their own food and their own kind along the way. They resented being barred from that. They didn't want to mix. White folks lacked not only color, but sense. They couldn't know God. Not with their tepid songs and whispered prayers. God was just some unpleasant check on their appetites. Their God was an unwelcome guest; a reluctant place set for him at the table.

As a boy, Jessie studied those pictures on the wall, and the huge four-poster canopied bed and the fragile white lace coverthings on top and the women who owned them. Those pictures, the places in them and this bed and that sheer white lace were his birthright, and these women his sagging, aging Sirens.

"You want somethin' to eat, baby?" Missy'd ask him with her honeyed lilt.

"He's not hungry Aunt Missy. We just ate."

"Don't tell me he's not hungry, girl. He can talk."

"No thank you," his little voice chimed.

"Bullshit," she said as she went off for ice cream.

"Missy, leave that boy alone," Ethel drawled.

Missy liked to pump him for information. She held his father in undisguised contempt and thought Lulene a fool for marrying him. She stroked Jessie's hair.

"You're such a pretty boy. You look like Mae." Mae was her and Ethel's sister, Lulene's mother, a noted hellion who considered her youngest her pride and joy. "Thank God you don't look like that ugly motherfucker your mama married."

Ethel: "Don't you talk about that boy's Daddy, Missy."

Missy went on in conspiratorial tones. "It'd kill Mae to see the way he treats Lulene. She had all kinds of men after her. Pretty men, not like that countrified thing."

Missy wasn't fond of men at all. For as long as anyone remembered, she had lived in that one bedroom with Miss Honey. It was never said, never mentioned. It was just "Missy and Honey."

Mr. Richard walked through the room. The only name Jessie knew him by, "Mr. Richard." A stooped old man, balding, round, and gray-haired.

"That ol' fool," Missy mumbled.

Whether he lived in the house, or in Ethel's apartments, Jessie never knew. In this world of women, Mr. Richard was the only man. He had something to do with Ethel. Perhaps an old lover, a current one, or even a legal husband. No one cared enough to say. Ethel would address him.

"You need somethin', Richard?"

"Jus' lookin' around."

Lulene spilled pleasantries. "How are you today, Mr. Richard. Are you feeling any better?"

"'Bout the same."

"Ain't nothin' wrong with that ol' fool but liquor," Missy grumbled.

"You don' know nothin' ol' woman," shuffling toward the door. Shanice passed him on her way in. He gazed suddenly at the ground and bravely stayed his course as she paused to regard him contemptuously. Big and florid, Shanice was a grand thing, an experience. Her girdles and hose hissed like vipers with her every step, her perfume overwhelmed you and her bracelets and spangles clanked and clattered in a righteous cacophony.

"What you doin' in here ol' man."

"I ain't doin' nothin'. You in here to beg."

"Shut up old man."

Her hair swooped and dipped, the big hourglass frame beneath it solid and sure. Those mighty hips swung wide arcs side to side in perfect time when she walked, like Fantasia's dancing hippos, all that woman tottering gracefully on two thin, tall heels.

"Baby," she sang as she sashayed to Jessie and took him in her arms, pressing him into her own full flesh, filling his ears and nostrils with her clanking and perfume. She caressed his face with the palm of her hand, her smile so luscious and enveloping it bordered on sinful adoration.

"Lulene he looks even more like Mama."

"Stop tellin' that boy he looks like some woman," Missy groused.

"You know I woulda brought you somethin' baby, but Aunt Shanice is so poor."

She darted toward Ethel. "Aunt Tee, I need some money."

Shanice always begged money. Like all black single southern women, Shanice taught school. They all did. It was the proper occupation for well-bred young ladies. To deal with children, with innocence, to lavish their gifts selflessly on them in a pedagogical setting should they bear none of their own, was de facto fulfillment of their biologically female function. Somehow she had borrowed and thrown together enough cash to buy herself a home, a nice two-story affair which suffered more catastrophe than any domicile should. Hurricanes tore the roof off of it, rising waters flooded it, termites gnawed on it like sluts chewed bubble gum. It probably sat atop a private fault line just waiting to shake it to splinters. These endless calamities strained poor Shanice's schoolteacher purse, but not as much as her love of frills and froufrou, lace curtains and round beds with gold and velvet headboards, baubles and spangles to wear, nectars and potions in which to bathe, and great big flashy cars in which to tote her great big flashy self. She never knew where the money went. She lived the way she had been raised to regard herself. Like a Queen.

"Don't you give that girl nothin,'" warned Missy.

"Aunt Tee, I swear to you it's for Little Mae."

"That girl got a houseful o' shit she don't need."

Ethel: "Hush up, Missy."

Well into her thirties, Shanice had done what no one expected. She had married. His name was "Smith." Just "Smith." No first name, no last. He was a contractor. That was good. He made "good money." It could have been the only reason for marrying him. That or desperation or the brink of madness. Smith did not speak. He mumbled. He sounded like Buckwheat on Quaaludes. An educated or refined man he was not. Clad always in T-shirts and work pants, he could be found laying on the sofa, sleeping, at all times. Most assumed she married him for free household repair service, of which she received much. That was a factor, but she also married him to have a child. Lulene and Shanice were both "illegitimate," quite a stigma in their day, and she would not curse a child of hers to a similar fate. It's hard to believe Smith was the best she could do. She probably just went about finding a father with the same planning and foresight with which she conducted her finances. He worked. He made money. He was potent. He was there. He would do.

Lulene insisted Smith was slow. "All that girl needs is an idiot child," she said of her pregnant sister. She prepared little tests for Smith, often involving Jessie. "Go ask him to read to you." Protest, protest. "Go on .

. . I want to see what he says."

"Smith," he chirped at the prone figure on the green divan in Shanice's house, "could you read me a story?"

"I'mawiltirerighna."

"Thanks."

"You see. You see. I bet he can't read!"

Despite his assumed illiteracy, Lulene was not above demanding free home repairs herself. He was a man. She might as well make use of him.

Throughout Shanice's pregnancy, the women feared for the child's looks. They feared the offspring would not rise to the family's demanding physical standards. They took solace in Lulene's case, however. Despite her husband's "ugliness," her children were quite lovely. Understand that to these women, "Ugly" and "Dark" were pretty much synonymous. Smith could have been, pound for pound, identical, but if he were light-skinned, would have been deemed acceptable. Shanice herself was "dark," a handicap in her relations' eyes. (Probably why she waited so long to marry, and probably why she had done no better than the somnambulistic, mumbling, illiterate Smith.)

The child "Little Mae" was born and was, alas, dark, but all admitted, cute. There was hope. Shanice fixed her fantastic attentions on the newborn, dressing her up like a Victorian doll in white lace and ruffles, booties with pink laces, bows in her three strands of hair. None were sure if Smith realized he had fathered a child. He'd pass the bassinet and peer into it, puzzled, as if a large fish lay wrapped in diapers.

Shanice "lived for that child." Smith was forgotten. Shanice never held him in high regard. It was assumed she suffered sex with him once. He now sank further in her eyes. Finally, she asked him to leave. He refused. He became belligerent. Ugly and useless she could deal with. Ugly, useless *and* belligerent—No. One day, while he—what else—slept, she took a lit match and touched it to the pre-flame retardant green divan on which he napped. He woke to blue and yellow dancing flames. As he swatted the flames like a swarm of bats, Shanice warned, "Next time," her child in her arms, "I'll kill you." He left the next day.

The women invaded Shanice's home, caring for the child, teaching it life's early lessons. Lulene took it on herself to teach the child her first word.

"Shit," she grinned, leaning over the cradle. "Say 'shit.'" Jessie tittered mindlessly, Janice scowled disapprovingly, and Talia grinned absently.

Shanice showed her love for Little Mae through food. The child soon grew fat. However, if it killed both Shanice and the child, she would be pretty. Her layers of fat were thus wrapped with frilly pink dresses and white patent shoes. At night, Mae sat attentive and dreadful on a kitchen chair while Shanice stood at the stove, hot iron comb stinking up the air over a gas flame. Shanice stood like a stevedore in the coal belly of a ship, skin beaded with sweat from the heat. Once the iron comb was sizzling hot, Shanice grabbed it and yanked and singe-combed the little girl's nappy hair straight and shiny, then bullied it into some ornate shape, Mae's face contorting with pain from the pulling and the burns. It was all for the girl's own good. For Pretty. Maybe if someone had worked on Shanice, she wouldn't have wound up with Smith. She wouldn't have grown big and spent so much on pretty things and envied Lulene her light skin and silky hair and for better or worse a man in the house, and children, honey toned and bright. The girl would be pretty, and merit the gifts of a pretty girl.

*****

"Blood!"

This was a greeting. Jessie's father, arm outstretched for a manly handshake, walked toward a prosperous looking man on this dusty cowtown street. Modest houses dotted the endlessly flat plain and the gray sky sat so low and angry it looked eager to crush them. The man's name was "Blood."

"Man you got too much money," Grandier yelled. "You gettin' fat." He laughed with his pink tongue peeking twixt his lips, air shooting past as if in failed whistles. Jessie hated that laugh. He counted the seconds until Blood's descent. He eyed the two hearses parked on the lawn, and wondered if corpses lay inside.

Prattville, Louisiana. Birthplace of the Grandier clan.

"Workin' hard. Workin' hard," Blood replied. "Ooh, and lookahere." Thus, it began. "This boy gettin' big.

Gonna be a football player. Hyech, hyech." The laugh sounded like a huge cat with a hairball. "How you doin', Junior?" If there was one thing he hated more than his father's laugh, it was being called "Junior."

"Nope. Not Junior," his father corrected. "I don' want nobody callin' him Junior."

"No lie."

"That's right. This is Jessie Grandier The Second."

"Ain't that fine."

"No. Not fine. I just didn't want no 'Junior.' It's right there on his birth certificate."

Jessie did have *something* for which to thank the man. "That's all right. I'll jus' call him Jessieboy like all the rest of 'em do.

Gee, thanks.

"Bet you beatin' off those little girls, huh?

Weak grin.

"Big ol' thing, too. You play football?"

Disinterested shake of the head.

"Whatchoo mean? Big as this boy is he don't play football?"

Sorry, Jessie thought, I know it's a racial imperative and all, but I'm so busy with my needlepoint I haven't the time.

"Bet you got yourself lots o' women. Just like yo Daddy. Hyech, hyech."

"Nope. Lulene's all the women I need."

"Where is that pretty gal."

She stayed behind because people like you make her puke.

"She's down at Ruby's."

"You tell her she better come on down and see ol' Blood. Come on in. Come on in. Marybelle wants to see you."

Jessie ached to see her again. The fattest woman in the world. And each year, each time Jessie came, she sat there, even bigger. Soon she would fill the house, her flesh popping out the windows and doorways. She and the house would become one. She would wear it like clothes.

That house was always dark, shades drawn, and thick with people. Blood ushered them in and Grandier greeted all the men sitting in the flickering blue light of a TV ballgame, up and shouting one minute, and sitting with a squish on the plastic-coated furniture the next. Jessie saw the women in the kitchen, as usual, cooking, pungent smells, heat and steam rising from their pots. And yes, all alone on a large, cushioned living room chair she sat. Marybelle, Blood's wife. The flesh rolled off her in waves and practically settled in fabric-like folds on the floor. Her upper arms were the size of hams, her legs like gelatinous tree stumps. It was like pictures of termite hives, the grotesque translucent queen too big to move. Her face was frozen in a mask of fat. He never saw her speak. She just sat there, and grew. Once, he accidentally walked through double doors at the back of the house and found dead bodies lying on gurneys. The men laughed at Jessie's mistake. The two hearses sat out front, waiting to collect more dead. Marybelle sat there, the enormous queen of of

Plattville's dead and dying. Blood was the undertaker, rich, his business good.

Plattville, Louisiana. Birthplace of the Grandier clan.

It was always Jessie, his father, and his mother. His two sisters stayed behind. The trips were made on Jessie's account. His father had fathered a son. Thirteen children in the Grandier clan, and he the only male who'd borne a son. These trips displayed the pride, the family's future—which Grandier owned. The trips were antidotes to excessive draughts of Lulene's kin, those uppity old yellow women who, Grandier knew, poisoned the boy's mind against the paternal clan.

They'd travel through the gleaming New Orleans airport to a dun-colored addition hidden out back, which housed an airline routed to places you'd rather die than go. He was sure Hell was on its itinerary, and feared that, to visit kin, his father might book a trip.

In flight, Jessie nursed a Coke while his father made vulgar with the stewardess.

"I flew better 'n this in Korea. Tthth. Tthth."

Lulene sat inscrutable and silent. Voluble and playful when alone with Jessie and her girls, she bore herself like a specter when with Grandier. She offered nothing.

Not even this airline went close to Plattville. They deplaned in some pasture, chemical plants looming huge in the distance, spewing smoke from shiny silver stacks, further antagonizing the low, angry sky. A car was rented and driven for an hour, for all of which Jessie pretended to sleep. The town approached when you saw the shacks. "Rustigold" Lulene called them. A color she invented—rust mixed with rotted wood when attacked by sunlight. Jessie thought them abandoned until he saw black folks outside, sitting on tattered chairs on porches, as if they'd waited lifetimes for a parade they'd deluded themselves into believing would pass.

This particular trip had special meaning. Jessie would view his legacy. The Land. His father always spoke of it. The Land in Plattville. Something he would inherit when Grandier died, and oh how Grandier loved to discuss what would happen when he died. "When I die, I don't want you to sell nothin' in Plattville." "When I die, don't you let nobody cheat you out of that land in Plattville," as if he would trade it for nylons and chocolate.

They drove through the poorest sections of town, the black parts of town, to arrive at Aunt Ruby's house. Jessie took for granted there was little else to Plattville, just shacks and broken-down clapboard boxes full of poor black people. Years later, on another trip, he found lovely tree-lined neighborhoods, large, well-tended lawns fronting fresh white paint on the large, Deep South-style wooden homes. Walking past he saw white people, something he had never seen there. He passed a store and entered. It was chock full of them—white people—and rare for Plattville, the aisles were well-stocked. He picked some items, paid for them, and left. Returning to Ruby's, she eyed the bag sharply.

"Where'd you get this?"

"At the store."

"You went over to Grayson's?"

"Yeah."

"All the way over there?"

"Yeah.

"There're places closer."

"I felt like walking. I just wound up there."

She paused. "How'd they treat you?"

He was shocked at the question. "Fine. What's wrong?" He didn't realize what the color line still meant down there.

"What?"

"Nevermind."

She paused. "It's real nice out there, ain't it?" she said, as if he had visited someplace she only read about in books. She hid a hint of steel in her voice, as if she'd spent a lifetime numbing herself to the fury that such things weren't available in her own neighborhood.

Ruby still lived in the Grandier home, where those thirteen had been born. It sat, a little faded but still acceptably intact, next door to a crumbling house which still held tenants, like hostages, and an overpriced coin-operated laundrymat, both of which Jessie's father owned.

Their rented car pulled up to the house, windows shut tight and air conditioner blasting against the heat and humidity. Ruby, her husband Darrell, daughter Tisha, and toddler son Dwayne gathered on the porch in greeting.

Stately, Lulene, shades on, stepped out of the car. A smile came on cue, and she waved. Once acknowledged, Ruby tumbled down the porch steps.

The women hugged. Stiflingly hot, wet air invaded the car. Jessie pushed the front seat forward and stepped out seeking relief. None came.

"You got air conditionin' an' everythin' in there," Ruby exclaimed.

"I don' drive *nothin'* but the best."

"Grandier," admonished Lulene at the boast.

"It's the truth."

"How've you been, Ruby?" Lulene asked.

"Oh . . . the flesh is heavy but the good Lord sees me through."

"How's Tisha."

"She's holdin' up."

Tisha stood on the porch with her right arm stuck to her face. The flesh on her arm was adhered to her face as if she had lain down to a languorous sleep and awakened unable to move. She had been burned. In that old house heat came from red hot coils. In the bathroom, in a nightgown, she caught fire. Doctors had fastened her arm to her head to graft new skin. She was about sixteen. Next to her stood Ruby and Darrell's only son, Dwayne, only four or five but already the most disgusting child on earth. His limbs were dotted with sores like freckles, open, oozing and red on his brown skin—mosquito bites, ant bites, cuts that he picked at and which festered. Jessie'd once seen him eat a roach.

"Jessieboy!" Ruby hugged him. She was big, like all the folks in Grandier's family. Jessie's father was the shortest of the men at six feet even. Ruby stood eye to eye to her twin. They looked nothing alike. He was a stocky, sharp-featured brown man whose every move displayed military swagger. Everything about her was soft, her features, her plumpness, her sweetened vocal tones. On her arm was a large six-inch scar, raised smooth skin half an inch across, stitch marks lining it on either side like train tracks. Even young Jessie knew no white woman, no moneyed man, would bear such a scar. No rich man's doctor would be so careless in his needlework. That scar defined her in his eyes. It wouldn't happen, he thought, in his family.

Since birth, Jessie'd witnessed two different and constructive modes of self-preservation: his father's military bullying, and his mother's suave intimidation. Grandier was fearless, cigar between two fingers, head jolting backwards in emphasis, the subliminal threat of physical force despite his mouth, from the first, displaying a hint of a victorious grin. Early on, Lulene learned the advantage of beauty, and took it. The exotic face, a bit Asian, maybe Indian, black, no one knew, couturier clones she made herself and wore like mantles, her manner polite, a trace distant, emitting the barbed fragrance of masterly control. As a woman, Ruby had learned none of the former; as plain, she could not know the latter.

There was a leper colony nearby. Her husband worked there.

During the ride to view The Land, Grandier and Blood talked old times and old acquaintances. They pulled off a two-lane road and jumped from the car. Jessie was loathe to leave the air-conditioned comfort for the stiff air outside, but followed. They stood facing a line of trees, about twenty feet of weeds separating them from a thick tangle of greenish swamp vegetation set in mud beyond which you couldn't see a thing.

"Here it is," Grandier announced grandly.

"What?"

"This The Land."

"Oh"

"I know it don't look like much, but it goes on all across there."

"Where?"

"Behind them trees there, Junior," Blood confirmed.

"Where?"

"All around there, boy!" Grandier insisted, testily.

"I can't see anything . . ."

"What's the matter with you, boy? All around here," Grandier assured, testily.

"It looks like a bog." Jessie blurted, incredulous.

"Goddammit boy, there are 100 acres a land out there. Look right between them trees there."

Seeing nothing more than swamp, he thought it best to nod and smile. It worked. The men looked down and beamed, satisfied.

Blood shook his head in wonderment. "All this gonna be yours someday, Junior."

CERTIFICATE OF DEATH
WASHINGTON, D.C.

1A. NAME OF DECEDENT – first	1B. middle	1C. last	2A. DATE OF DEATH	2B. HOUR
Lulene	Jones	Grandier	10/17/71	0052

2. SEX	4. RACE	5. DATE OF BIRTH	6. AGE
F	Negro	12/21/38	38

7. BIRTHPLACE OF DECEDENT	8. NAME AND BIRTHPLACE OF FATHER	9. NAME AND BIRTHPLACE OF MOTHER
New Orleans, La.	Willie Jones New Orleans, La.	Beatrice Francois New Orleans, La.

10A. CITIZEN OF WHAT COUNTRY?	10B. IF DECEASED WAS EVER IN MILITARY SERVICE GIVE DATES	11. SOCIAL SECURITY NUMBER	12. MARITAL STATUS
U.S.A.	19__ TO 19__	534-58-1331	Married

13. PRIMARY OCCUPATION	14. NO. OF YEARS IN OCCUPATION?	15. EMPLOYER	16. KIND OF INDUSTRY
Teacher	12	City of Washington, D.C.	Education

17A. USUAL RESIDENCE	17B.	17C. CITY OR TOWN
10426 Branwell Dr.		Wheaton

17D. COUNTY	17E. STATE	18. NAME AND ADDRESS OF INFORMANT
Montgomery	Maryland	Col. Jessie Grandier – husband 10823 Bucknell Dr. Wheaton, Md. 20902

18A. PLACE OF DEATH (ADDRESS)
Walter Reed Army Medical Hospital

19. DEATH WAS CAUSED BY: (ENTER ONLY ONE CAUSE FOR A. B. AND C.)	20. WAS DEATH REPORTED TO CORONER?
(A) INTRACRANIAL HEMORRHAGE (B) due to or as a consequence of: CEREBRAL ANEURYSM (C) due to or as a consequence of:	YES

21. OTHER SIGNIFICANT CONTRIBUTING CONDITIONS NOT RELATED OR GIVEN IN 19	22. WAS OPERATION PERFORMED ON ANY CONDITION IN 19?
HYPERTENSION	Yes

23. WAS AUTOPSY PERFORMED?	24. I HEREBY CERTIFY THAT DEATH OCCURRED AT THE HOUR, DATE AND PLACE STATED FROM THE CAUSES STATED. AS REQUIRED BY LAW I HAVE HELD AN (INQUEST – INVESTIGATION)
Yes	Investigation

25. CORONER	26. DATE	27. DISPOSITON	28. NAME AND ADDRESS OF CEMETERY
Brian Olin	10/21/71	Burial	Arlington National Cemetery

Chapter III

SEVENTEEN

The L.A. County Marshal held a notice he didn't have to read. Jessie took it as it was offered, impassively, and shut the door. He had approximately three days to pay the back rent or leave the premises. Fearing this daily, hourly, living with it like a butt blister for the past month, he examined ads in the back of the weekly free paper with headlines screaming "EVICTED?" which promised to delay homelessness for a fee. The fee was hefty. It should have amused him that you had to have money to be as poor as he was, but amusement would have required panic, which he was two or three steps beyond.

It was not fair. He'd done with the booze. He'd got through all that, only to face this ultimate humiliation, this irrefutable confirmation of his innumerable personal failures. Laid off, and now eviction—homelessness. He'd called home to beg for money. He'd gotten the expected response.

"Why is it," he wondered, "that so many others needn't stagger unshielded against the gales of this life?"

"Because they," he answered himself, "are not you."

He hadn't asked for much. He didn't want my father's life's blood, or even his affection. Just his money. It was the only thing the old shit had worth wanting, and the only thing he wouldn't part with.

He looked around this place in which he had lived for five years, his first one-bedroom apartment and no, there was not much to show for it; not much worth keeping. On the eve of his first raise, he bought some furniture. He knew not eating on the floor meant he was "A Man." He must have rearranged the stuff six or seven times before he settled on an order. He took pains so that the speakers faced the sofa, on which he lay, and played some songs he loved.

I'll be waiting quiet by your side
You can turn away, won't hurt my pride
I'll ask you again
You'll sit back and pretend
It won't matter

There wasn't much to move. He called Mark, a friend. The son of a Nebraska minister, he had come to LA about the same time as Jessie, landing a job with a TV production company to face a meteoric rise, of which Jessie never admitted his jealousy. He was one of those "young men" whom people "adored," and took to themselves like a son. His words seemed always disembodied, second hand, mainly due to a profusion of borrowed humor, sitcom straight lines, standup schtick. His sincerity sounded so grave one suspected artifice, but that wasn't so. "If there's *anything* I can do . . ." he said.

At night, like thieves, they carted big boxes to Mark's compact, and drove back and forth to his garage where the belongings would be stored until Jessie could claim them. Until he was back on his feet, the logic went.

He called Sally, who he had known since age fourteen. They met in junior high. She had been a short, round girl, a 4'10" butterball of Jewish rage and hilarity. They were both members of "The Family" back then, an ad hoc group of friends, dear friends, of like age and mind, whose parents all worked in the DC beltway government industrial complex, more like family than friends.

She made an offer; so he drove the badly limping Datsun, a secondhand wheel that didn't quite fit, suffering under the weight of even his few belongings, down the winding canyon road to Sally's, where he arrived, evicted, exhausted, not broken, but badly and seemingly irreparably bent. They had grown up together.

[*Back then. Seventeen*]

Five years after his mother's death, late one warm summer night, Jessie and "The Family" hopped in a car and drove from their suburban Washington, D.C. homes to Annapolis, Maryland. There, Sally and Emily had summer jobs as counselors at the bayside Habonim Camp Moshava, a socialist Zionist camp for the spoiled children of massively bourgeois, typically capitalistic Americans, who, being Jews, owed this sop to Israeli-style Kibbutzism.

They had to pull over every fifty miles or so so Archie could piss, get back in the car, guzzle more of his six-pack—imported of course—belch, then demand they stop again, threatening to soil the Volvo, which was "provided by a grant from the Moe and Beverly Weinstein foundation."

That had been more than fifteen years ago. He remembered when he hadn't yet <u>lived</u> fifteen years. He had forgotten them. No, not forgotten, but the memories never came. He never called them. Like Lulene, they were the past. Done. He didn't need them.

Jessie often found rich, spoiled Sally in her bedroom closet, in which she had placed a chair to read. She invited him in, but would not come out. In there, she couldn't hear her mother, Elaine of the Muumuus, forever sedentary in the kitchen, whip thin, chain-smoking, expressing disapproval, nor the cold joviality of Good-Time Morty, her father, ready with a joke, a genuinely good-hearted man who had long ago abdicated his place as father, and assumed the less taxing role of breadwinner.

Adults were rarely seen or heard. By sixteen, once they drove, their homes became occasional crash pads, their parents automated teller machines, years before the advent of the same. They were my Family. Clandestine runaways only they didn't have to run. Their parents beat them to it. To Jessie, they were safe harbor. They were Home.

Archie, belching farting Archie, spoke with a mild British accent and though probably immaculate, bore the air of one who rarely washed. His physicality consumed him, his overtly confused sexuality obsessed him; the sort who'd piss anywhere, roadside, front lawn, brick wall, he didn't care, while the others whined in protest, rolled their eyes and hid. Tall and gangly, he leaned down and said, "It's a *natural bodily* process," hands deep in pockets, obviously arranging his improperly placed member.

"He's got a point," John the level-headed would say, cocking his head in thought.

The school intellects, Fichte freaks, the Smithsonian mall in the afternoon, Georgetown coffee shops in the evenings. Each one a little adult, with car and cash and social agenda. No playing. Outings, yes, daytrips, but no playing. No high school things, no sport events and proms and parties. They'd congregate with Scrabble board and wine, and talk of later days when they'd have grown to matter.

Emily, half-girl, half-woman, pouty child-face and womanly breasts, dated short and skinny John the level-headed of the Prince Valiant haircut, Dumbo ears, and comical nose. A pretty girl, they cut an odd figure, but hey, it was love. He got cute once you knew him. The daughter of Jungian analyst who later lost his license for seducing male patients, Emily wore kerchiefs on her head, sandals on her feet, and knew the words and tunes to all of Bonnie Raitt's white-girl blues.

Grumpy Ben Weinstein planned to be an architect. His pale skin seemed always dry and flaky. Bone thin and short, his face perpetually screwed into a scowl of exasperation and dismissal, he berated Archie for his vulgarity, Sally for her materialism, Emily for her spaciness, Humanity for its stupidity, respected John, and feared Jessie.

Someone should have warned him. A stranger should have passed him by and whispered, "Remember this. It may not seem so, but it is so important." He might have listened. He might have. To him, back then, those times weren't real. Later. Always later would his life begin.

Someone should have told him.

At Habonim Camp Moshava, they parked in the woods, almost a half-mile from the camp, about which Jessie was not pleased.

"I didn't sign up for a nature walk here."

"I suppose you'd like us to carry you?" Ben asked.

"Oops, forgot the litter," Sally added.

"It won't hurt your bourgeois ass," Archie drawled, "to walk for once, instead of color coordinating which car you'll drive to school with your ensemble."

They marched through the wood, Jessie, city born and bred, convinced that lions and bears lay in wait, the silence eerie. They walked, hearing only breaking twigs and dried leaves beneath their feet, and Archie's urine, probably melting things it touched.

Jessie saw his shadow, and looked up, expecting streetlights. "Moonlight, asshole," he heard.

An owl sat in a tree, the light shining off its feathers, looking right at him.

The bark of trees seemed white in the moonlight. Each step brought the soothing sound of wood and leaves, crackling, rustling. A wind tossed the treetops, a sparkling spray of the littlest bells.

They came to the clearing on which the camp sat, near the Bay. The long wooden structures edged a clearing. The buildings were all screened, pouring light onto the darkness between them. The moonlit night, these dark structures, the quiet night sounds brought visions of dark rites going on beyond those lights. The light was sinister, the darkness only comfort.

The camp kids had just finished playing "Capitalism," a regular camp game in which, prior to dinner, they were given fake money and told to purchase their food. The dinners were priced far beyond their means so they all went hungry. Abusive, but to the point.

A long, tattered rowboat lay grounded on the shore.

"How do you drive this thing?" Jessie asked.

John: "Ben does. Ben will row."

"You don't *drive* a rowboat," Ben spat.

"Don't worry," Archie added. "*You* won't have to do anything."

Sally: "Is it too late to go shopping?"

"You're disgusting," Archie said. You could just feel him ready for a socialist rant. He climbed unsteadily into the boat, having consumed about five beers. "You people make me sick with your cushy little bourgeois notions."

"Shut up, Archie," muttered Ben.

"No! How do you sleep at night knowing your goose down comforter comes from your father throwing people out of their homes so he can build rich people's playpads?" he said to Sally.

"She cries herself to sleep," said Emily, laconic.

"Keeps me in shoes," Sally yelled, laughing.

"Doesn't that bother you!?" he demanded.

John: "What's she supposed to do, Archie, run away from home? Live in youth hostels?"

"Yes!"

"Oh yeah. And you with a house full of original English carvings, which you practically lick every time you walk in the door, and your private room full of toys."

"I didn't ask for them."

Ben: "He salves his conscience 'cause he doesn't have to ask for them, but he takes them. All bought with the money his father makes building bombs."

Archie grinned sheepishly, " . . . Well . . ."

"Is this thing safe?" asked Jessie.

"Oh!" Archie raved. "Doesn't know how to act if he's not in a car."

"Kiss my ass Archie."

"You're just as big a bourgeois shit as anyone here," John accused, "and let's not talk about cars the way you sing the praises of Mercedes corporation."

"Yeah," Emily added pointlessly.

"I appreciate fine craftsmanship, that's all."

A collective groan.

Ben took the oars and quiet ensued as they rowed slowly into the bay. The water still, Ben skillful, a soft swishing as his oars rhythmically disturbed the water.

"My ovaries hurt," Sally offered.

Jessie: "Gas."

Quiet.

Rocking the boat, Archie struggled to his feet. "What are you . . .!? Siddown asshole! Arrchheeeee!" all in unison. On his feet now, the boat threatening to capsize, he mustered all the dignity he had.

"I have to urinate."

"Jesus!"

"Catheterization is a painless and surprisingly economical process," Jessie offered.

Sally: "He's gonna turn this thing over and we're all gonna die."

Daintily turning his back, all heard the strong, obviously prodigious stream smash into the bay.

Emily: "Impressive."

The Chesapeake Bay is a significant shipping channel, hosting multiple vessels at any given time, so it should not have surprised them when the mile-high lights of what looked like the worlds largest ship bore rapidly down on their tiny, unlit, completely invisible rowboat.

"OH MY GOD!"

"AAAGGCCHHH!

"It's no big deal," drawled Archie, so maudlin drunk death would have been a blessing. Ben simply twisted his face in disgust at such squeamishness to mask his panic as he frantically rowed the boat out of harm's way, his stick-thin arms pumping furiously, sweat beading on his brow, visions of never built architectural masterworks dotting his vision like proverbial concussive stars.

*

They gravitated toward water on their outings. Assatigue, Great Falls, Rock Creek. They went canoeing on the latter, choosing heavy wooden canoes over the more temperamental aluminum, being less than expert boatsmen, and not realizing that the several mile long row-way was dotted with locks, heavy wooden mini-dams around which they would have to carry the boats. The things weighed a ton and the carrying of them frayed fingertips and tempers. Jessie earned the wrath of all by refusing to board unless any living non-human thing—"Ant, spider, rhinoceros, I don't care . . . get it outta there!"—was removed from the boat each time it was set in water. Bugs grossed him out.

Tall trees and smaller bushes lined the creek densely enough that Jessie imagined himself on a trek through uncharted waters, on his way to dark, mysterious places. John and Ben manned the oars. They floated at a stately pace.

Seventeen year-olds make foolish and beautiful sounds on the meaning of life. Jessie tried to remember what they thought of themselves. He tried to remember what they thought would find them with time and age. He couldn't. They had floated this far, and imagined they would do so 'til they died.

Emily lay back, eyes closed. Her gauzy cotton dress fell limply around her, like an exhausted friend. A womanly girl, she kept herself to herself but insisted on the primacy of the here and now. She loved John. When he was gone she thought of his smell, she said, and a particular vein that bulged through the skin of his penis. She thought of it and smiled.

Archie with a beer in his hand, drunk, immersed in his insatiable wants, maybe needs—justice, sex—things he never found in the right proportions. Thinking he would find them elsewhere. Thinking where he might go, where they might greet him warmly, like family.

Sally and home. Mom and Dad, her sister and the man her sister married and didn't even know she didn't love, parents with little time or patience for children and Sally tethered to them like a horse to a barbed-wire post. The endless little hurts that dotted her days like periods.

Ben thinking it all so much trouble. The yelling and screaming back home. The older sister he loved, who had read poetry to The Family last night and enthralled them all. Wanting simplicity and unclutteredness, and willing to sacrifice everything, and later, everyone for it.

John, the gentlest of them all. Probably knowing it wouldn't last but too kind to tell a soul.

And he, remembering Lulene, remembering that one year that stuck in his memory, that he hadn't bludgeoned to little more than a blur. Not realizing he missed her deeply. Not knowing that he loved them all.

After rowing for hours, they reached a clearing, an incongruous pond, still and eerie, in the middle of which stood a rock formation with a skeletal tree poking ominously from it. They stopped. The others swam in the still, murky water. Jessie and Sally sat on the bank, sure they'd catch anthrax or plague should they swim. The wet ones parked themselves on dry land and they all sat in silence.

You couldn't imagine a way back from here, this place so far away, so still you imagined yourselves the first ones here and the last who'd ever see it.

No one would find it again.

Won't you hear a word I'm trying to say
You know I'll never walk away
If it hurts you let me know
I'll keep trying, even though
You won't let me…

Chapter IV

MAN THINGS

The intensive care/post op ward sat in a quiet section of the third floor of Walter Reed Army Medical Hospital. The smell of disinfectant was strong, the walls a light shade of military green. The near empty corridors echoed with occasional sounds, heels clicking, a door opening, a gurney rolling past.

A nurse walked three well-dressed children down this quiet hall and then disappeared behind a door. Inside the room, a patient lay motionless and unconscious. Machines monitored her heart rate and other vital signs. The patient's head had been shaven prior to the operation, and was now wrapped in white bandages. A tube ran into her mouth, taped in place, connected to a machine that mechanically pumped air into her lungs. Bottles hung by the patient's bed, which dripped intravenous liquids and antibiotics into her body.

"Mommy?"

The younger daughter approached the bedside.

"She can't hear you," the nurse softly informed her. This daughter remained silently at the bedside.

"You can come closer," the nurse told the other two children. She had been told that this was the last time the children would see their mother. The older girl, Janice, stepped forward. After a pause, the youngest boy also stepped close.

"She's in a comatose state right now," the nurse explained. "Her brain activity is minimal. Her heart is beating very, very strongly. She has a very strong heart. Her brain activity is so weak, though, that she is clinically dead. She can't hear you. It's just a matter of time now."

On Jessie's tenth birthday, the Grandiers were living in the Maryland suburbs of Washington, D.C., and had a back yard to themselves for the very first time. In a rare show of interest combined with insight, Grandier feared for the boy's masculinity. Grandier worked long hours and had little to no contact with the children, save to beat them on Lulene's orders if they had misbehaved. She would try to do it herself, but her attempts were so half-hearted, her frustration so complete and befuddling, her wits-endedness so discombobulating, that she became comic, like some cartoon blue-haired schoolmarm gone completely loco. The kids feigned pain, only to collapse in hysterics once she left the room.

Grandier was much more efficient. He had not yet sunk to the point where he inflicted pain in revenge, on the children and the wife who should have loved him, who knew they should act like the ones out there, somewhere, on TV, but refused from spite or hatred, for the loneliness he hadn't the words to articulate or the means to remedy. At this point, he would come home, conference with Lulene while the kids waited. Post-conference, he approached them, glum, clad in the deep green uniform with the little odd-shaped pendants and multi-colored insignia. To this day none of his children could properly identify them. To him, it was their duty as children of a military man, a duty they shirked, probably, he thought, out of disrespect for him and the service to which he gave his life. He considered the slight as he anticipated their punishment. First, he stated the offense.

"Your mama tells me you went out when she tol' you to stay here and do your chores."

The children lied. "We thought she meant to do the chores later."

"You tellin' me your mama's lyin'?"

"No. No. She misunderstood."

"It's not her job to understand."

Whap! leaning over the bed they'd get it on the butt. Unpleasant, yes. Crippling, emotionally or physically, no. Not yet.

Observing Jessie, Grandier didn't like what he saw. Shockingly small for a boy in his family. Didn't play ball. Still grabbed his mama's skirt. Should have come to his daddy by then, talkin' about Little League and Cub Scouts, fishing trips. That's what boy's did. When Grandier'd walk by and tousle the boy, or roughhouse, he would screw up his face, bat the hand away, and run. There was hope, though. He wanted a dog. Good. A boy thing. Like Lassie.

Lulene hated dogs and swore she wouldn't have

one in her house. "Filthy, stinking, shitting things" she called them. She protested for weeks, but finally relented. Jessie wanted a Husky puppy, one that would grow into a huge white fluffy dog. He'd read stories of them saving lives in the frozen north.

"I know a fella can get anything," his father boasted.

Grandier spoke to his "fella" who promised the dog within a week. Three weeks passed. One day, home from school, Jessie saw a strange man in the house— huge, fat, gut covering up his belt, the shirt buttons stretched to the point they might shoot loose like bullets. He wore polyester head-to-toe, red polyester slacks, white patent shoes and matching white belt, and a see-through sea green polyester shirt with elephant ear collars. Fashions by Maurice of the Ghetto. This did not bode well.

"The dog's right downstairs, tied up outside."

Jessie ran to the basement and out the back door, and there it was. A mutated pig. As big around as a sewer pipe, little legs that looked about to crack from the strain of all that girth, a combination of brownish, yellowish and greenish fuzz coating its body, which Jessie feared might be mold. It looked about to die from old age.

"But I wanted a husky," he whined.

"That *is* a husky," the Fella informed.

Lulene came down. "Oh my God!" she muttered, hand to her breast. Jessie looked plaintively at her, and she put her arm around him.

"That's a good dog," Grandier said.

"It's not what the boy wanted," Lulene told him. "He wanted a puppy."

"This is better. You don't have to teach this one nothin'."

After more absurd exchanges, the fella took the dog back to the probably abandoned junk lot on which he had found it.

Another fella took a stab, trotting out four pups that looked like Dobermans crossed with lizards.

"No!" Lulene said.

Strumming through the paper, Grandier found a puppy sale in a nearby suburb. Collie/German Shepherd. That sounded nice. Jessie and his father hopped in the car to purchase a dog.

"Can you come, Mommy?"

"Nope," Grandier said. "This is a father/son thing."

"I'll let it in the house, what more do you want?"

For Jessie, being alone with his father was always hell. He had nothing to say to the man, and found it hard to look him in the face. There was no active loathing. Just distaste. He found him . . . vulgar. He lacked refinement. He was always sweating. He'd grown chubby, a little jowly, and clamped cheap cigars between his teeth that smelled like shit. Too often, his eyes were red and his breath smelled of sour liquor. They sat in silence.

"You know your Mama doesn't want no dog in the house."

"Yeah."

"But I put my foot down. 'My boy wants a dog!' I

told her. And I want him to have one."

"Thank you."

"But you gotta take care of 'im. You got to train him an' clean up all his mess."

"I will."

"It's a lotta responsibility."

"I know"

"Son, I gotta tell you I was glad you wanted a dog. Every boy wants a dog. I wished I'd had one when I was a kid."

He detested being told what "boys" wanted and did and how they acted, as if there was a manual he had misread. He was heartened when they pulled up to a well-tended home. It minimized the chances of a junkyard mutt or mutant mongrel. A woman greeted them.

"I came to get My Boy a dog," his father announced grandly.

"We've got plenty," she amiably replied.

The mama and papa dog were on the grounds so the prospective purchasers could get a gander, the mother a full-bred Collie, the father a handsome German Shepherd. In a playpen frolicked seven gorgeous brown and white pups just eight weeks old. Frisky, playfully biting each other's heads, they delighted the group of kids and parents reviewing them.

Circling the playpen, Jessie spotted something odd in the corner—a tiny motionless ball of black and white fur being trampled by the frisky pups competing for the visitors' attentions. He moved closer. Destiny. Neurosis.

Call it what you will. You read about it in dime store paperbacks. You hear it in cheaply sentimental songs. Two beings' fates entwine and they will spend some of their days together. Doubtless their end will be sad; but no force on earth or beneath it can stop them from seeing it through.

Black and white, brown spots along the sides of its face, it was unlike the others. The runt of the litter. Eyes like agates. Eyes for him. The others flit from one thing to another, each sound, each body grabbing their attention for microseconds. This one looked directly at him, and its gaze didn't wander, even as it laid its head back down.

Jessie stuck a finger through the diamond-shaped playpen netting to stroke its head. Its little pink tongue emerged to lick the finger. The puppy stood, and stumbled closer to the netting, closer to him, before it fell back down. He reached down into the pen and picked it up. It looked at him for a moment and rested its head against him. It seemed very, very tired.

"That dog looks sick," his father said.

"I like this one."

"Boy what's wrong with you. All these healthy dogs all around here and you wanna take that little one."

"I really like it."

"Look at these others, they all alike."

"This one's special."

On the way home, the dog lay lifelessly in Jessie's lap. Petting it, he could feel the bones beneath its coat. Fleas crawled along its fur that it didn't bother shaking or picking away. He was happy when his mother said it was pretty.

"I think he's sick," Jessie told her.

"I don't know what's the matter wit' that boy. All these dogs runnin' around and he picked out the runt."

They tried to feed it but it wouldn't eat.

"We'll take him to a vet," Lulene said.

The doctor gave instructions for care and feeding. He didn't give it the standard shots. He said to wait on that.

Jessie and Lulene covered the floor of the upstairs sewing room with newspapers. They coated the dog with drug store flea powder, watching innumerable ticks and fleas fly off and die. She couldn't believe such a little dog could feed so many. The dog didn't protest. It just sneezed softly and repeatedly. Jessie went to the kitchen and painstakingly prepared the feeding formula according to the vet's instructions. Again the dog refused it. Lulene found an eyedropper. Jessie held the dog while she dripped the food slowly into it.

He was shocked that she helped him. She stayed in the room with him and stared at it, stroking it, teasing it, trying to get a rise out of it. She said it looked like her Uncle Henry. She said it had his eyes, the same expressions, that it looked at her the same way; and she said it without irony, in such an earnest way it made him shiver.

She wasn't one to revise a virulent and unreasonable opinion. She cared for that puppy like its private nurse. When Jessie nodded off, she saw him to his bed. When he awoke, he found find her in the sewing room, caring for the beast. Two weeks later when they took it to the vet again he asked, "Is that the same dog you brought in a couple of weeks ago?"

"Of course," she told him.

"I could have sworn that dog would die. I figured why waste these folks' money on shots."

She was glad to hear that. She had converted to Catholicism in young adulthood, having discovered a pressing need to hear her fate's dissonant tune, and acknowledge her spasmodic little dance to it. On entering a cathedral for the first time, this young life-long Southern Baptist breathed the incense-stained scent of ritual, stately processions trudging their way toward some certainty, and she joined them. She applied her fatalism to many things, and this was one of them. To her, this dog was right.

When the pup was up and around, playful and hungry, Talia, Janice and Jessie thought up names. Scouring an encyclopedia, they found "Caesar," and it was done.

Soon, Lulene had made a song.

> "Caesar Caesar shittin' on the floor
> If you don't stop all that shittin'
> You won't be Caesar no more."

Within months of buying the dog, Grandier got orders for Vietnam. Jessie feigned sobriety while singing inside. The girls and Lulene did the same. The family would move to New Orleans so Lulene could be near her family. Caesar got big overnight and took to wandering. He'd jump the low brick fence outside and take adventures. Coming home from school, Jessie would spot him rambling down the alley with some dog friends, sniffing and pissing. Seeing Jessie, he broke from the pack and slowly walked toward him, head sheepishly hung, tail wagging apologetically.

Grandier and Lulene flew to New Orleans to buy a house. The kids protested they were old enough to stay alone for one week, but Grandier brought his sister Iris up from New Orleans to babysit. Fifty-ish, squat, she forever stood with hands clasped in front of her, feet together, fingers locked, like a bad diva about to belt a showtune. She lived in housedresses with tiny floral prints and fuzzy slippers in a variety of hues.

First thing in the morning, she grabbed the local DC newspaper, sipped her coffee, and read the obituaries. Jessie couldn't figure why she'd read local DC obituaries. She knew no one in town. Back home, it might have made sense. At her age, friends would be dropping like flies—but here?

"Looky here. Forty-five. Heart attack. Not much ol'er 'n Baby Bro." She called Grandier "Baby Bro." "Eleventh Street. Where is that?"

"Near the Capitol," Jessie answered.

"Musta been a colored man."

She wore bad dentures she continually clicked together—little arrhythmic clicks as if sending messages to no one in particular. She cleaned continually. Asked to treat the trip as a vacation, she spent it with dustrag in hand, and pushing the vacuum, clicking about the house in that housedress and slippers, tsking at the clothes the children wore to church, or the fact of their election not to go in their parents' absence, or their general slovenliness, all because God wouldn't approve. She believed in Jesus, living her life for a future, heavenly reward. The "Good Lord" as she called him, would save her, see her through, take her Home, give her strength.

Back home, she attended the funerals of strangers. She scoured the newspaper for a service at a nearby African Methodist Episcopal Church, hoping it would be a good one, one in which the temporality of life was outweighed by grief and pain borne by the living at the loss of one so dear.

At the good ones, soul-stirring speeches held forth endless promise for her own approaching ceremony, promise that men and women would weep, that the preacher would rave magnificently regarding her goodness and rightness with God. The bigger the fanfare, the more meaningful the life. The living of it, the mistakes, the horrors, the crimes—they could all be erased if the funereal roof was uproariously raised.

She lived in a New Orleans shotgun house. They called them that because the houses were so long and narrow, you could shoot a gun through the front door and kill everyone inside. They were poor folks' dwellings now.

With Iris, in hers, lived her brother Huey, he of

the glass eye so big it looked like a child's tea saucer compared with the tiny, puffy, liquor-reddened slit of the other. Forever on the front stoop with a cheap bottle, other drinkers with him, little black kids with hair shaven to their skulls running about and playing, creating a constant clamor on that narrow street. Huey disappearing when Grandier came to visit, to avoid displaying his mangled self—their mutual shame.

Iris's husband Bertrand lived there, too. Wheelchair bound, he barely moved. He couldn't walk or speak. God only knew if he could think. Mabel fed him and clothed him and washed him. Huey did the lifting and the carrying.

Bertrand scared Jessie, sitting immobile in that metallic chair, just a tiny tremor in the hand and the open eyes to tell you he was alive. Raised Catholic, Jessie thought they must have done something horribly wrong to be burdened with poverty and broken or useless bodies in that ramshackle house. He knew nothing at that time of bad luck and living in it.

Jessie had heard a story about Bertrand and Iris, one of the endless horror stories he heard about that family, but this one stuck. They said that Martha, the oldest of all the Grandiers, lost her mind over Bertrand. She went mad when Mabel took him from her, the story went, and spent the rest of her life in a mental institution. Grandiers wielded the threat of "illness" in the family. Whenever one of them misbehaved in another's eyes, the first was warned that he or she would go the way of Martha. Lulene said that Martha was the only one with any sense. Trapped in that little dusty cowtown in a house full of petty, mean men and women with no way out, no real hope for anything better save marriage to some local man who'd wind up drunk or mean, at best dead, leaving you with a house full of children wanting this and needing that. Martha got out. She chose the peace of four walls and her own bit of quiet. Sometimes, Lulene said, that sounded better than Grandier's world.

Old photos lined Iris's fireplace mantle. Bertrand had been a dapper man in his day. He was lighter skinned than Mabel, a catch she thought. He wore ill-fitting suits, cheap imitations of the day's styles. These pictures weren't like Ethel's. Hers were immortalizations. These were prisons that mocked the dreams of those within them. That's why the pictures seemed odd. Hard years blared through the airs of young men and women, years mocking the smooth flesh, years and trouble like hobgoblins at their shoulders, laughing at them.

Lulene would take her children to New Orleans, to her own people. Grandier away in Vietnam, there'd be none of his clan to nose about and talk their silly-talk. Grandier wouldn't be there to demand they be what they were not, to scream because they were not his TV-fueled dream of what a family ought to be.

The day finally came, another moving van called—about the sixth move Jessie'd endured in his ten years. Things packed in brown boxes lay all about the floor. White moving men smelling of sweat towed boxes to the enormous van. In the past, all of this should have promised something new, but in fact just meant a change of particulars, specifics, the basics remaining the same, the insular household slowly, year by year, wading a little deeper into its own muck and mire. This trip was different, though. This time would be different.

*

In the car, Caesar rode in Jessie's lap almost all the way from Washington, D.C. to New Orleans. The women took a plane while Jessie and Grandier drove down with the dog. Caesar was bigger than Jessie but loved to sit on his lap. The window rolled halfway down, he rested his dog-chin on the glass, his long snout hanging out of the car, his long hair flailing in the wind, tongue hanging out, dripping drool on the windshield. He loved car rides. At first they rolled the window all the way down, but then he jumped out at every stop sign to stick his nose up the nearest woman's dress and scare the shit out her. That dog always wanted to run and explore every sniffable crotch and fire hydrant within a thousand mile radius. He got what he wanted when he stuck his head out of the car like that. He was free and moving and he could really feel it. Even when he dug in his heels, four legs peddling so fast they became blurs, his body so close to the ground it almost scraped against it, even then he couldn't run that fast, not fast enough to compare to this, wind and air whipping his head like lashes, eyes squinting trying to take it all in, drink up every sight and sound, on the lookout all the while for other dog-flesh while Jessie loved the watching of it.

Throughout the trip, Grandier talked of Man Things. "You gonna have to be the man o' the house while I'm gone. You gonna have to take care o' your mother and sisters." All three were big enough to stomp him into the ground.

Jessie and Caesar had a kiss. Jessie'd pucker up and the dog would lick his lips, then his ear until it tickled so much Jessie couldn't stand it any more. That dog knew him better than anyone. When he was sick or sad, Caesar would lay his head on his lap and just look at him, knowing. That trip with his father wasn't bad at all. Days on the road passed like ordinary time.

"We need to have a Man-to-Man talk," his father said, sitting on the edge of his motel bed. Jessie dutifully sat on the edge of his own. "How come you don't ask me things? Other boys ask their Daddies things."

"Like what?"

"Ask 'em to take 'em to ball games, and teach 'em how to build things . . ."

Jessie sat mutely. He'd been forced to attend a football game with Grandier. It was 30 degrees in the sunshine and they sat so high up and far away that even had he been interested—had he not been freezing to death, cheeks so numb he dribbled huge chunks of the potato chips he tried to chew, had his feet and hands not been so numb he could have been crucified and felt nothing—he might as well have viewed a particularly sportsminded antfarm.

Grandier and his buddies drank beer and talked intimately of the black players, their personal lives and professional skills as if they knew them and had had them to macho tea the afternoon before.

"That boy got too many women, that's his problem," one of them said. "He ain't got no stuff lef' for the game."

"You see that car he drive? That thing big as a house, and gold, look like some pimp car down on 14th Street."

"He a country boy."

"A *rich* country boy!"

"See Sonny," one of them said to Jessie, "that's how you get rich."

Grandier felt proud that he personally knew some baseball player nicknamed Blue Moon or Mill Dew or something. The guy played for a Major League team. Grandier had had him to the house. A genial fellow he seemed to Jesssie, not bombastic or arrogant like most of Grandier's friends. He gave them free passes to a game. It was warm enough that Jessie mustered acceptable enthusiasm, standing when the crowd stood, cheering when the crowd cheered.

"Ask him to autograph a ball for you," Grandier said. Jessie didn't want to. He didn't want an autographed ball. Displays of idolatry annoyed him. Were this man excellent, that excellence should have been accepted as the expected, with silent admiration. When the subject of the player's prowess arose, little baseball fans should have muttered "extraordinary," accompanied by knowing nods and appreciative half-smiles. Drooling, fawning, and clamoring for scraps of flesh or locks of hair was simply vulgar.

"What's wrong witchu? Any other boy'd kill for an autographed ball. He can get 'em *all* to sign it for ya'."

After the game, Mill Dew went to dinner with them. Jessie was quiet They drove the ballplayer back to his hotel. Mill Dew said his goodbyes and went inside. Grandier didn't drive away.

"You know, Son, I'm really disappointed in you. There isn't a boy in the world who don't *idolize* ball players. Now you go up there an' ask that man to sign a ball for you."

Jessie trudged slowly through the glass double doors and into the hotel lobby. He tried to think of ways to get a baseball he could write on himself. Adults standing in the elevator smiled down at him. "You wouldn't happen to have a baseball on you?" he thought.

He stepped from the elevator into an endless corridor filled with floral wallpaper, gold-veined mirrors and globe-shaped light fixtures hanging from the ceiling. Trudging past door after door, staring up at the numbers, he tried to think of what to say. He imagined that Mill Dew would be as embarrassed as he.

"Hi, there." Mill Dew said as he opened the door.

"Hi. My father suggested . . . I mean I wanted to ask if you could sign . . . a ball."

"Sure." He smiled. "Come on in." Jessie stared at his feet. Mill Dew rifled through a bag and came up with baseball, then found a pen with which to sign it.

They were silent for a moment, but Mill Dew stole glances at him.

"I got a feelin' your daddy might want this more than you do."

"Oh, no . . ."

"Don't worry," he said. "You seem more the studious type to me. I bet you're good at school huh?"

Jessie shrugged, nodded.

"You get good grades?"

"Yeah."

"That's good. I think your daddy wanted to play ball when he was younger. An' if I remember right, he wasn't any whiz with the books. Here you go." He handed Jessie the autographed ball.

"Thanks." Jessie shook his hand and turned to the door.

"You stick with the books, okay?"

Jessie shook his head. "Thanks."

"Didja get it?" his father asked as he opened the car door. Jessie showed him the ball.

"Good. I'm proud of ya, Son. Now you have somethin' to show your friends. Now they'll really believe your Daddy knows Mill Dew Otis."

Jessie wound up keeping that ball.

The new New Orleans house was a simple three-bedroom, one-story affair (a lot of New Orleans houses are planar, sprawling outward not upward since the place is below sea-level and the water table is right about your knees) near Pontchatrain Park, a well-kept, middle-class, black suburb. It had a massive back yard with a couple of big, healthy, full-grown trees in it that Jessie could climb.

Two blocks away sat a long, shallow ditch. White people lived on the other side of it. Blacks crossed it to walk to school or church, but they didn't live on the other side, and the black children didn't play there.

The new Catholic church was the pride of the Diocese, built in the shape of the cross with a huge crucifix of the bleeding Jesus hanging over the centerpiece altar. On Sundays, blacks entered from one side, and whites from another. Black faces filled the left "leg" and "arm" of the cross shape, while whites filled the "head" and the right appendages. Parishioners filtered out of the same doors through which they entered, socializing, kvetching, eying one another's outfits. A black priest stood outside one set of doors, and a white priest outside the other.

Jessie attended a Catholic school, "Our Lady of Extreme Unction"—dubbed "Our Lady of Perpetual Hip Motion." The school proved a good one, attracting students from both sides of that little ditch.

Petunia Beauchamp lived next door. Divorced. Her children attended the local public school. Her son Johnny took Jessie to her bedroom, dug deep in a dresser drawer, and pulled out 8x10s of his mother being fucked. Jessie was transfixed by a gaping beaver shot. She had spread her labia lips to their extremes, and the cameraman got right up in there for an incredibly disgusting shot of what looked like a hideous gaping-mouthed monster, dripping some viscous, probably greenish juice from its liver-like lips. In other shots, her huge tits flopped sideways, the enormous dark nipple areas nearly touching the sheets. Insertion shots were favored, the large anonymous penis slipping into her quite juicy hole, the large anonymous penis slipping into her mouth, the large anonymous penis slipping into her doggie-style. Jessie was amazed. Johnny's interest was principally sexual, while Jessie wanted to know what manner of shutterbug would take such pictures, and what manner of exhibitionist would pose for them. He'd overhead whispers about his father screwing Petunia. He wondered if that was his father's dick in those pictures.

Jessie was straight out of the East Coast then and spoke with the appropriate accent. The locals spoke with New Orleans twangs turning "oil" into "url," and speaking so slowly you could have clubbed them to death while waiting for the point. He couldn't understand a word they said.

Within three months, the family was loaded in the car, taking Grandier to the local Army base to catch transport to Vietnam. They all stood dutifully by as the plane took off, then got in the car and giggled themselves silly. Lulene got stopped by a cop.

"Okay. Quiet!" she said. "Look sad. Cry."

"Yes, officer?"

"You were goin' about seventy there Ma'am."

"I'm sorry officer," her voice trembling with emotion. "My husband . . . we just took him to the base. He's going to Vietnam. I'm upset. I . . . I guess I wasn't paying attention."

The officer looked in the car to see three sad-faced children. Janice had produced tears, one of her talents.

Pause.

"Okay, Ma'am. Go ahead. Be careful."

They all maintained glum faces until the threat had surely passed.

Breaking the silence and into a smile, Lulene said "White people," as she often did when confronted with naugahyde and Dynel wigs and other useless things, "are so smart."

*****

Lulene Mercedes Jones Grandier died on October 17, 1971, in Walter Reed Army Medical Hospital in Washington, D.C., of complications arising from an aneurysm located in a blood vessel on the lining of her brain. On their last visit, her children had seen her in a private room in the post-operative intensive care ward. Corrective surgery had been aborted when the patient's blood pressure rose dramatically, causing the aneurysm to burst, flooding the cranial cavity with blood, while depriving her brain of oxygen. Corrective procedures had been taken, but her brain had been asphyxiated long enough to cause permanent damage. To continue the operation would have caused her death. The procedure was aborted.

June 20, 1986

I saw this woman on the bus. She had one pale, sickly-looking child on her lap, and another sickly child across the aisle from her. Both children wore baseball caps, but the hair peeking from beneath the caps was sparse and wispy. They had hard, encrusted patches on their legs and necks that wrinkled their skin and made them look like little old men. They looked like they had cancer. A children's hospital sat right on that route. One boy looked right at me when I boarded, his legs kicking back and forth, too small to touch the ground, arms wandering akimbo, little boy eyes taking in this and that. I felt sorry for him. I wondered if he would live, and if he knew he might be dying; and it's silly, the refuse of some sci-fi daydream, but I wanted to hold him, and have the power to outrageously delight him, just once, for a little while.

Some cells grew angry and monstrous and started eating him alive. Every week that kid whose own insides attacked him sat before a big machine that shot rays into him, while doctors, who set leeches on people years before to suck out tainted blood, hoped the rays would kill those malignant things that had grown as acquisitive as the humans they lived inside, confusing survival with domination, and like us, just desperate to survive.

Those kids just got in the way, that's all. Those poor little shits just got in the way.

Chapter V

HOOTENANNY
(or)
More Man Things

After six months in LA, Jessie found his own apartment. He'd landed the mailroom job at the major television network for which he would work for several years. Now, with a steady income, time came to move on.

"You should look over there," his cousin Alma said, referring to the neighborhood around the corner from her house. When he told her he was looking near work, in the Hollywood area, she warned, "They'll never rent to you out there, boy. Whatchu wanna live out there for?" as if the place were geographically remote and under South African law.

Just driving through Beverly Hills adjacent, he saw the sleek young men. They walked the street in fewer clothes than he had been raised to consider proper. They flaunted arms that looked like artists' sketches, the sinews beneath the skin prominent, calves like melons, luxuriant, thick thighs coated with fine, sparse hair and formed with an unnatural skill, silky torsos that gleamed in bright sunlight, the insolent nipples on firm chests like harlots' painted moles.

During a college summer in New York, he swooned less openly at wonders of a headier sort. Yes, he noted the clones swaggering in skin-tight jeans and aviator shades, but the ones that made him ache wore huge linen shirts that billowed when they walked. Worn jeans teasingly hinted at the almighty legs and thighs. Sandals on their beautiful feet exposed the perfect little strands of hair marking the upper digits of their long and lovely toes. Artfully unkempt hair attuned only to the wind's governance, and the leather bags on shoulder straps doubtless contained manuscripts. They darted purposefully through doorways, urging him to follow just by being so goddamned gorgeous. The ones that glanced at him and smiled, a glint in the eye, and the big teeth flashing as they ran by, he could have clubbed them and taken them hostage, to hold close and kiss and hold until he wore them to their bones.

Lulene was a very good Catholic. Regarding "fairies" or "queers," she promised to kill any son of hers should he turn thus. Jessie took her words to heart and from an early age, squelched any and all sexual stirrings. By age ten, he had chosen the priesthood as a career. It was the natural the choice of Papist gay males whose mothers adopt the church's penchant for emotional forceps and other less subtle dissuasions. That is why his Catholic schools were lousy with priests and Jesuits who, in between self-pitying, week-long drunks, slaveringly eyed young men's thighs and buttocks.

This dam of sexual feeling sprung a leak in his mid-teens. Lulene years gone, churchgoing had been abandoned, a fact about which Grandier whined with righteous Christian heartbreak, despite the fact that he hadn't darkened a Baptist doorway since the Jurassic.

Jessie'd developed a passion for reportage. He'd taken to reading semi-highbrow periodicals. Yes, he thoroughly enjoyed the high levels of wit and insight in the articles. But major selling points were the ads in the back. A California clothier called Male, Inc. placed ads for undergarments on the last few pages. Ads of men in skimpy drawers, jockstraps, and panties of varying revealing cuts, all the models formed brilliantly, their hair coifed within an inch of its life, sunken cheeks, pouty lips, and worldly eyes promising decadent bedroom acrobatics. Jessie would study every inch of those men, down to the obvious bulges in their raison d'etre, and then retire to the basement to masturbate. Never a television addict, he took to watching shows with dual male leads, buddy stories, where weekly one male faced life-threatening gunshot wounds/diseases/ mental collapses, demanding that the other touch/ hold/fondle him and declare undying (platonic of course) love. Cop shows and westerns were the most reliable. He longed to be wounded and held like that, a strong hand to stroke his head, the feel of a rough face against his own as the kiss of concern was laid on his forehead. Dwelling on it, dreaming of it, he retired to the basement to masturbate.

But he never acknowledged the sexuality of it. The wanting and wanking was just an animal burp; it had nothing to do with him—inside—which was far above it. He had a dream of breaking into a thousand little pieces and flying off with a passing wind. At night, he would lie in bed and consider that he would die someday. He'd think of what it might be like to simply not exist. He'd think of the moment before, the instant before he died, knowing his eyes would close and would see nothing, ever again, of this life. It scared him to think so, but each night, like ritual, before he closed his eyes to sleep, he took himself to that brink, to that moment before he would no longer be. This world held nothing for him, he knew. The transcendence of it was all he could seek, the only thing in which he would find comfort or home. He wasn't yet sure of the "how," but distance from things corporeal was a start, his indifference to things carnal.

Throughout college, those thoughts remained, as did his distance, the steel that both alienated those around him and drew others to him. He'd found his method, in beauty, in art, the books he read and the music he heard. Through those, and only those, he faced the eternal, not in the art itself, but in the names that had managed to successfully hide their humanity behind it, and rang like churchbells and hung in the air just as long.

ELLINGTON   BACH   THREADGILL

MINGUS   VERMEER   PYNCHON

BARTOK   ELLISON

Immortals. Ghosts both more and less than men whose vaporous forms in sound and image would walk the earth until someone or something reduced it to rubble, who'd haunt the young and old as relentlessly as any ghoul in any horror show. They were grand in that. Grotesques. They'd done what no being should and given God the finger, the bastard who'd have them rotten and forgotten like any vermin in any field.

He yearned to flaunt the laws of God and be adored for it by men who hadn't the skill or nerve to do so themselves, as he adored those he so admired and feared he would never reach. To follow Bartók's journey from searching classicist, to mad pantonalist, to master whose music encompassed, so sweetly, every nuance of the lives he lived, without a trace of bitterness, with an abdication borne of knowing he would die, and that it didn't matter—the music had given him that. It had given him the wisdom to speak like battered old grandfathers in fairy tales, Prosperos, full of sorcery and sorrow.

Wisdom. He would become old, and he would gain more than his earthly share.

For years, he had been "The Writer," starting back in fifth grade when his teacher Miss Tuddle crinkled up her little pinched-faced beak, yanked her bifocals even lower on her nose and said, "Hmmmm. You just might have something here." At home he got Grandier saying, "What you doin' sittin' 'round here doin' nothin'?" He'd be reading at the time. "Why don'chu go out an' play some ball or somethin'?" At least he no longer insisted on "playing ball" with him. That ended one year previous when Jessie, forced practically at gunpoint to a grassy field to lob a baseball back and forth, took great aim and fired the ball past his father's glove, directly into his solar plexus, knocking him backwards and windless. The man stumbled home gasping.

Jessie continued writing in high school, and his forays through semi-highbrow periodicals led him to edit the high school newspaper, where he installed Family members Archie, Sally, John, and Ben on his staff as various writers and editors. The articles were written during all-nighters, and the days spent ditching class in the newspaper office, out the window of which they'd climb and drive off to enjoy a tasty Georgetown lunch. By then, Jessie had decided that he was, and would be, a Writer.

You must understand that back then, the word still meant something. *The Word* still meant something. Some like Barth and Pynchon were sages. Others like Leary or Thompson, madmen. The mythics like Kerouac sowed romance in teenaged heads like poppies in Dorothy's field, through which, drunk, the Family ran until the drug caught them, and brought them to their knees. They had all grown up on the tail of the '60s, not old enough to fear the draft or death in a rice paddy, not old enough to take serious drugs or threaten anyone's established order, but old enough to see it, and young enough to dream that it meant something, that actions so bold, so portentous, would undoubtedly be remembered always, and lead to nothing short of a revolution in the way they lived.

They were raised in a time—or maybe they just misconstrued the time to be one—in which an idea had value, in and of itself, and could be a mighty force. There was no time for the "television machine," as they derisively called it, and they were so removed from the daily mundanities that trips to supermarkets left them giddy with mirth. The bright lights, trippy muzak and stacks upon stacks of multi-colored food and auxiliary items stacked floor to ceiling, aisle after aisle, seemed the epitome of the ridiculous. They had constructed a world in which such things had no place.

Jessie enlisted in the English department at Harvard but did not last long. When awakened in a poetry seminar to discuss the outrageously irritating Wordsworth, he dismissed the poems as, "full of exclamation points," and when the associate professor, in all seriousness, suggested the topic would make a lovely thesis paper, he left the department. The cold, clammy death-infected entombment of what should have been life-affirming and beautiful he could not bear. More than that, the writing did not satisfy. It wasn't good enough, and he feared he would never get it right. He considered film to bypass his own mind's eye, that unforgiving thing that showed him nothing worth seeing in his own writing, and focus instead on actual visions and façades. And once he had sat in film class to watch real pictures and laugh, honestly laugh, and was asked to consider and wonder at his laughter, he was hooked. This study still had life. It breathed the open air instead of that crypt-stench.

Film it would be. In those dark rooms he imagined himself up on that screen. He imagined himself a life worthy of projection. He favored the mythmakers, those who, behind the camera or in front of it, painted themselves so large they were consumed by what they created, suffocating within stockades of their own imaginings. We're talking Welles and Keaton, Dietrich and Davis. They recreated themselves just like he always wanted to, because then this world couldn't touch him. It would be up there that mattered, and this, down here, in three dimensions, would be the penance he would pay for that shaft of light projecting pieces of him up there. Only the penance.

Mind you, nary a camera did he touch. "If God had meant for me to lug an Arriflex," he stated, "he would not have created cinematographers." His self was the skill to be honed, not focus nor f-stop. He sat in dark rooms and watched images flow and saw detail and design that few will ever see; he learned to see frames as letters and scenes as words, each work a tome, in glyph, to be painstakingly deciphered.

Thus, he found himself the summer of his sophomore year, at NYU, in a film writing course, this temporal carnal world he so disdained for so long pursuing him like a supernatural shock-film demon, watching the collegiate boys and the worldly men flash their gifts at every turn until he knew he couldn't stand it anymore. And so this nineteen year-old virgin got himself laid.

Yes, there were the crowded Village bars, some

with ferns, where professional men hung out in their blue jeans and button-down shirts, but they seemed too public for his purpose, too . . . overt. Lurking Catholicism demanded such acts transpire in private, in the dark, clandestine. A crowded place off a main street, where one would walk out to face more crowds and traffic going about their daily routines, no . . . that would not do. There would be sex on the mind when he entered and left, illicit sex, and this veneer of normality, of the everyday, would not do. There should be darkness.

He had wandered to the waterfront one bright afternoon and found decrepit beauty there. Abandoned rail tracks alongside the dirty river, the rotting wooden canopy overpass casting huge shadows, wooden docks jutting out into the water, old buildings down to skeletons now, like delapidated sculptures. There was a ghostly peace there, just the occasional car overhead. Hungry gulls squealed. People dotted the scape. Moving closer, he saw some sunning, some reading, some wandering in and out of the skeletal structures.

Closer, he saw that most were men. Male sunbathers lay nude on the wet, creaky wood. He saw others, shirtless, through the lattice of the buildings, alone and in pairs, on the second and third floors.

That night, that night he couldn't stand it any more, he headed to the waterfront. There were bars there, darkened streets outside them, harsh shadows instead of bright streetlights, hushed voices, not raucous laughter. He walked there, down dark streets on which he probably could have been killed, but not caring, or not caring more than he needed, finally, after years and years of wanting and dreaming—by no means more than he needed. Remember, Jessie at nineteen years old, had never been touched, could only imagine what it felt like to run his hands along another's flesh, to feel lips or warm moist breath on his own skin. After a point, desire overwhelms, most waking hours consumed by it. Exposed flesh becomes like fire and yourself a desperate self-immolator. He was prone to priapic episodes. On subway trains and crowded buses, in class, his jockeys filled to bursting with a hard dick unnaturally twisted by the tight-whites, demanding freedom and leaking big dollops of sticky, anticipatory juices.

His heart pounded as he walked down Houston. He felt the pulse in his neck, the thump and whoosh of blood rushing to his head. He felt it in his fingertips, little rhythmic pumpings, as if the blood stomped and raged inside him like a spoiled child denied. It was the revenge of carnality. It took satisfaction on having been denied by this heartless, heady little shit for so long.

That first man was a tight jeans/plaid shirt-wearing mustachioed thing of thirty-two years who tottered a little on his cowboy boots as if they were spikes, hips swinging side to side like an on-call streetwalker. The lisp wasn't too noticeable, and he was tall, and broad, with a chest full of furry brown hair.

By accident, Jessie'd found a place not too threatening. It wasn't too dark inside, and only one huge fellow was posed at the bar wearing leather chaps and leather vest. The rest of the clientele looked rather harmless. A small dance floor sat in the middle of this bar, which was too small to have a dance floor of any kind. When dance floors shrink to postage stamp dimensions, they become pathetic, and those who dance within them, even more so. Mercifully, only one man danced, and he shirtless, rapidly twirling two enormous silver fans in elaborate patterns, up and down, before and behind, looking more like he was juggling angry pigeons than anything else.

The crowd was sparse, and few took notice as Jessie entered. He crossed to the bar, where a large, bearded bartender approaching middle age leaned toward him and stared, eyebrows raised, awaiting his order. "Bud," he blurted, despite the fact he rarely drank and hated beer. Paranoid, he was sure that bartender's looks said, "We don't want your kind here." Luckily, he smoked, but feared, while lighting up, that he resembled a rebellious deb who'd stepped into the girl's room with her gum-popping friends to trash the ball.

Standing alone against a wall, cigarette in one hand, Bud in another, wearing round frameless glasses with wire rims, a long-sleeved button-down shirt, and fashion fatigues, he knew terror when he noticed the large man in leather staring at him from the bar. Soon, however, the cowboy booted one tripped toward him, big smile, and said, "Hi there, never seen you here before . . ."

Within fifteen minutes they were outside hailing a cab back to his place. The man expressed dismay at heading home by midnight, man in tow. He admitted it usually took till three and four a.m. To avoid offending, Jessie stuck with monosyllables, principally "Yep."

"You from out of town?"

"Yep."

"You wanna go back to my place?"

"Yep."

Of the man's Village apartment, Jessie would always recall the air of gauzy rose and fuschia—fringed lamps, Erte prints—and a dozen pairs of cowboy boots lined against the wall. The fellow talked of his window dressing work, and of his friends, the last time he hit the Island. Jessie knew this bored him, but had no idea the content was cliché. The man could have recited "Hiawatha" in Urdu for all he cared. He was there for sex.

First, the kissing. Jessie'd only felt familial pecks on the cheek. He'd never felt his own lips on someone else's. This one attached his face to Jessie's and opened his full wet lips to fill Jessie's mouth with a great big ol' tongue, and the warmth and wetness pulled Jessie closer, to tighten his arms around the man and feel his own tongue touch the stranger's and dance. When the mouths parted, Jessie rubbed his face against the man's to feel the flesh against his own. The stranger put his hand to Jessie's face, in a gesture so open and warm and welcome, Jessie closed his eyes and leaned his face toward the open palm to press himself against it.

This was what he had read about. This was what all the abstruse talk that knocked against him and off again, refusing to settle and sink in—this is what it had all been about. Flesh and skin. The heat and silk of it, the warmth and fragility, that most feeble of shells pressed against another and never getting close enough, never feeling warm enough, the sonnets and songs of want and need—and he didn't know how he lived so long without it.

Chapter VI

LIFE DURING WARTIME

After Grandier left for Vietnam, the year in New Orleans became a good one. Caesar had grown up to be a big, strapping dog. He had a huge yard to run in now, and places to run away to and play. Lulene taught school, kindergarten, as always, but didn't worry about someone coming home, maybe mean, maybe drunk. She had friends and they'd go out together. One night she got drunk. A friend brought her home only to have her dash to the bathroom and puke prodigiously. Janice and Talia were horrified. They pushed Jessie into his room so he wouldn't witness this family shame. He thought it was funny.

Lulene fixed up the house. She relaid the floors with the help of relatives, built an addition onto the house. She saved up some money and bought things for the place. For the first time it was if she had a real home, and she was happy there. She sat with the girls by the sewing machine, showing them stitches and hems. She helped Jessie with his homework. Janice developed her penchant for student councils and the like, while Talia had her first boyfriend, a sweet-natured, dull fellow of whom Lulene approved entirely. They'd sit on the living room sofa together, while Jessie, Talia's friend, and a boy from across the street spied on them, wondering when they'd kiss. They never did, or at least they were never caught.

Grandier made tapes. Instead of writing letters, he sent audio tapes, and with Lulene, they sat around the living room and listened to them. In return, she had them make an answer tape to send to Vietnam. At the end of each tape, Grandier said how much he loved them, and that he missed them. He sounded sincere. It was during this absence that Jessie pretended he loved his father. It was noble to do so, romantic, the wife and children at home while the military man fought abroad. It was a role he could play, and play well. He liked the sound of it. He liked saying his father was away in Vietnam.

Sometimes, at night, Lulene let him sleep with her in her big bed. He slept in Grandier's T-shirts. They fell below his knees. He said they made him feel close to his father. Lulene liked that. She repeated it to Grandier when tape time came. She told all her friends what he said. It was the epitome of wartime suitability. They all reveled in their respective roles.

It was a year full of normal things—outings, dinners, squabbles, visits, thoughtless days that bled into one another, the green lawn outside with the big trees, often climbed, the neighborhood children playing outside, the afternoon rain in summer, like clockwork, flooding the streets, ending abruptly, the fluffy black clouds skittering off like pranksters, the yellow sun returning, amused.

They were all quite happy.

It was the year Jessie remembered—the only year of his youth he would not omit. It was the year of his childhood.

*

Jessie prayed to the silver crucifix hung on his wall, trying to reach a God in whom he fervently believed, begging for the single favor he had ever asked for, forswearing any future requests if this one would be granted.

His oldest sister Janice had won a silver crucifix in school. She gave it to Jessie and he hung it on his bedroom wall. In itself it was pretty, and its symbol was still potent to this eleven year old. Janice knew he prayed each night. He told her so. He prayed each night. For the first time he made up his own. For fear a lack of form would dilute his message, he bracketed his ad-libs with Our Fathers and Hail Marys. During the ad-libs, he begged the crucifix to let his mother live.

When he walked in the house, he felt something in the air. He had learned to do that—to gauge the emotional temperature in the house, in the room, to determine the level of danger. Upstairs, he heard voices in his parents' room. There, Lulene lay on the bed, a cloth on her head. Her face bore a pained expression so immoderate it seemed ridiculous, feigned. Grandier's eyes were red, his nostrils flared. He'd been angry. Janice had tears on her face and Talia had the peevish look of the suburban cheerleader she was.

"What's wrong?" Jessie asked.

"Nothing. Go back outside," Janice said.

"What's wrong, Mommy?" He walked toward her.

"Leave your momma alone, boy," Grandier said.

He moved away. "Mommy's sick," Talia finally answered.

Something had happened. A tense standoff, with Lulene lying on the bed, hand on forehead in a near comical Camille. No one spoke. They all watched her, awaiting the next move, and wondering how explosive it might be.

"Let's go," Grandier said, grabbing the jangling key ring off the dresser and walking from the bedroom. Talia and Janice breathed sighs of relief. After a moment, Lulene gathered herself off the bed as if every lift of every limb was torture to her. Talia and Janice helped her downstairs and into the long, brown Buick Electra 225 with the white vinyl top that Grandier had pulled to the curb.

Later, he learned that Lulene had developed what seemed an unbearably painful headache while in the car with Grandier. He'd taken her to the Army Hospital, where the young doctor suggested she take an aspirin, lie down, and wait for the headache to pass. She insisted that this was unlike any headache she had suffered, that it was too severe, but the doctor assured her that headaches sometimes took such forms. Driving home, her pain increased, and she insisted on returning to the hospital. There, another doctor repeated the words of the first. It was after these trips that Jessie found them home.

She had always been too prissy, too high and mighty for Grandier's taste, with her imitation designer dresses and her light skin and straight hair. He always knew she thought she was better than him, that her people were better than his. On the way home, she started in again, on Army doctors, about how he should take her to a real one, as if those who treated him weren't good enough for her. She had the reputation even in school, at Southern University, the pretty yellow girl who talked to few and said "no" to all the boys. Most of them stopped asking. That's when Grandier moved in. In his uniform, head of the ROTC on the campus. This was back in '52 and the ROTC didn't take just anyone. A colored man was somebody in the ROTC. And she was pretty. God she was pretty.

"What that yellow girl want with a black, country thing like you?" his friend asked.

"Jus' wait," he told them. "You jus' wait."

Catching a girl like her wouldn't be bad for a country boy from Plattville. He was the youngest of them, but the undisputed head of the family. *He* was the one that sent their Mama money. They said Lulene was smart, too. She had the grades. They called her uppity because of the way she talked, not like a New Orleans girl, but like she came from back east somewhere. All those older brothers and none of them with a son. She would make some damn good kids. The ones who got somewhere in the Army had wives. If they asked him why he wasn't married, he said straight out that he hadn't seen a woman good enough.

He knew what to do. Everyone on campus knew him, just like they knew her. He made sure they got time together. He flattered her. He wooed her. He made sure she knew how big a man he was and how big his plans were, and that it would take someone special to keep up with him. She saw her ambitions mirrored in him. She grew to trust him. After a while, she admitted to him that the man who raised her wasn't her real father. He understood. She was illegitimate. Tainted. Then he surprised her. He said he didn't care, while making clear that any other man would. He may have been a "black, country thing," but she was a bastard. He would overlook her sins if she would overlook his. To a nineteen-year-old illegitimate girl, this was a kindness. A year and a day from their first meeting, they were married.

"She's in a comatose state right now," the nurse explained. "Her brain activity is minimal. Her heart is beating very, very strongly. She has a very strong heart. Her brain activity is so weak, though, she is clinically dead. She can't hear you."

Chapter VII

LOST IN THE STARS

Before Lord God
Made the sea or land
He held all the stars
In the palm of his hand
And they ran through his fingers
Like grains of sand
And one little star fell alone

— Abbey Lincoln, "Abbey is Blue", Riverside
Records, 1959

Los Angeles

"The weather forecast was issued at 10:30 a.m. The forecast for Los Angeles and vicinity . . . heavy winds and warm high pressure continuesto dominate, with temperatures in the upper nineties on the coast, to 110 in the inland and valley areas."

Hot air, like worms, swarmed all over you as you stepped outside. A burning wind rushed around like a frantic child, forty miles an hour, whipping your hair and clothes to disarray, wanting to dry the sweat that formed so fast it didn't have a chance. It made the national news. Photos of sweaty highwaymen and traffic cops, animals dipping themselves in public fountains, pigeons panting all made the morning papers. It hit 102 in the city. The air turned brown from the smog. The mountains, so resplendent in the cool clear fall days, you couldn't even see.

It seemed like madness. In the early evening, the

sun lowered itself, long shadows cast, and your mind and soul said you should be cool, the day near its end, night coming on, sleep. But the hot wind still blew, old newspapers took wing on the blistering gusts like in apocalyptic nightmares, the burnt orange sky enraged, casting a gorgeous hellish glow on everything beneath it.

It scared you. No terror, just unease, because you knew that anything could happen—and just about everything does—and you knew that anything could happen to you—and just about everything has—with more of the same to come. Sometimes you're forced to stare the world in the face and know that it's not on your side, that it doesn't care about you. It'll prove it sometimes, especially in LA. The hillsides will catch fire because they want to. The earth beneath your feet will tremble and roar and shake to the ground everything you've built on it. The sky will get angry and throw hellish hot gusts at you all day and all night long.

It all wore the long, flowing robes of sadness. The kind of sad you get when illusions fade, and you're just a person in a mind and a body in which you will always be, alone, and a little lonely, because that is what God intended, and that, all said and done, is not so bad. On hot nights he walked alone and felt the beaded sweat on his skin as the wind brushed it. In times like this he saw, with neither blinder nor mirage, dreams nor visions, the world that lay before him, and how lovely it could be.

On hot nights they hung out of windows and lounged on front stoops. The brown women fanned themselves, some children on their laps, others asleep in their arms, the men off together, drinking beer, watching the younger girls walk by in their halter tops and short skirts, the Dells on a car stereo begging, "Stay in My Corner." Kids ran up and down, screaming at nothing, while the elders talked in softer tones, harsher accents, the rough dialect pouring from their mouths like bullets from a tommy gun. On nights like this, Jessie loved them all. They knew the street, had a sense of it, didn't fear it or the night, and had the guts or foolishness, all animal and warm, to do it, whatever it might be, in the wind and the ungodly heat, to talk and sweat and fight and drink and hold their babies in their arms all out in the frightful air like everything else under heaven.

On nights like this, Johnny went to a bar called the Detour. Local men, mostly older, went there. Even the ones his age looked older. Hard use. He liked the ones with beards. He'd stare at them. Just stare, with a little half smile on his face, his back to the bar, his elbows on the bar behind him. The pose was laughably coquettish, but it worked. They knew what he wanted. They'd sidle over to him, big and broad and plain, stand real close and smile down at him. They'd ask his name. They'd crack some joke and as he laughed, they'd grab his butt. He liked that. He liked it mean and rough.

He needed them, the tall ones, the fat ones, the thin ones, the ones who looked like they'd make it hurt some. They had to want him. He had to feel their rough beards, and hear them grunt and feel their sweat as they plunged into him, while he watched, a thousand miles away, afraid they might reject his ill-toned frame, afraid they'd touch his hair, and feel the webbing, that he was bald, twenty-eight and bald and ugly, and wanting so badly to be of the young and the wanted that he bought some hair and bought some clothes and learned the stance and joined them. Even if it wasn't real, there was the illusion, and he could make an even trade, laying there sweet and passive for men who called him "buddy" and slapped his butt. Unmuscled, balding, ugly, he was still a young treasure to jaded men who lived for who they'd had and who they could get, and now, too old to change, not able to get as much.

Sweating, they wailed their loudest and the muscles spasmed up and down their bodies, limbs twitched and jerked and then slowly settled as they lay against each other, deep breaths, the residual shudders, the closed eyes that make need and want last.

"It's a balmy night; and I hope all you boys and girls are keepin' cool. It's the kinda night for walkin' hand in hand with someone you love. That's right. For those of you who aren't in love, here's a song that'll sure make you remember when you were; only here, only on KDMY, 103.7 on your FM dial . . ."

The Lord God hunted
Through the wild night air
For the little lost star
On the wind down there
And he stated and promised
He'd take special care
So it wouldn't get lost no more

1949

On one of those ungodly hot mornings, Kurt Weill sat in his Los Angeles hotel room. Echoes of war laced with a radio static hummed in his head despite the real sounds of leaves rustling in the trees and hissing sprinklers satiating warm green lawns. The War had ended five years ago, but the only sounds he had heard of it came via airwaves, for he had fled long before.

At the Bel-Air Hotel, the water from the sprinklers arched and shimmered in the heat and sun, dancing colorfully before settling on the ground. In the past sixteen years, he had traveled from the stately and old, fleeing its illness, watching it heave, and finally vomit all over the world, to this bright and vivid heat, dry as dust and sparkling new, like gold.

This bright and shiny, brand new

world, in all its gangly youth . . . of all the twists and odd contortions his life had made, that he would stand here in this Bel-Air Hotel thinking money and death was the most fantastic. He had returned to this white-hot place to drum up money, a deal, a contract on what had just died on Broadway. He considered a vow never to return after the bitter taste his last bite of Hollywood had left, but here he was again, all for the money.

The momentous had occurred to him that morning, like the most innocent of notions, like a small craving for a morning biscuit. That simple. The heat had awakened him. He was sweating. The sheets stuck to him. Walking to the window, the violent green in the bright morning sun sharpened every angle to a razor's pitch. He stared out the window at the brightness, the violent colors of the planted gardens, so hot already, so still outside that the trees and every blade of grass quivered with expectation.

And suddenly, he knew what everything was waiting for. For him. They had a message. That this was near an end; that no more notes would pour from his pen; that he would no longer make the chords dance, no more sit to ponder them, and find the one, that with the words, could break a human heart.

It shocked him, that he learned this in the heat of Bel-Air, in the glare of a sun so foreign to his very soul that he might as well have been on Mars. He smiled. It seemed absurd that something so momentous should attack him here. He who'd placed some bags in his car and driven from Berlin in '32, leaving behind all the books and the things, and even Lotte. How few who walked the streets or drove alongside knew that he was fleeing the wreckage of a conflagration that had barely yet begun; he was leaving his life behind.

At the border, seeing the sentries, seeing their guns, he left the car and those few links to all his life, and he walked, like a Sunday stroller, across, and from the other side, looked back: suited soldiers, sentries, keeping all the embers in, so they could grow hotter and burn, bright and strong.

He had thought of Lotte, who would make her own way. There had been no tears, no clinging to him or vows to be by his side. She simply nodded, and said she would make her own way. Not even the satisfaction of the weight of this moment. So matter of fact. "Yes we will leave our lives and loves behind but I must meet you there, so frightfully busy, some things I really must do."

"Don't worry. I'll meet you there."

Those words rang as he packed his bags and wondered where she was. Was this a love affair? Right then, he needed a love affair.

No. It was just theirs. And he would soon die, as he had discovered on this white hot morning imagining news of years-old wars as water drops on palm plants sizzled through his bedroom window in the bright heat of the Bel-Air Hotel.

Now man don't mind if the sky grows dim
And clouds come over and darken him
As long as the Lord God's watching over him
keeping track how it all goes on.

Inside was unbearable. The sun had pounded the building all day and the walls themselves gave off heat, even with the sun long gone. The wind still raged outside, whipping palm fronds from their anchors and hurling them like multi-bladed spears. He couldn't sit in the stifling indoors while those winds still blew.

So Jessie walked.

He walked up and down the hilly, winding streets lined with houses and apartments, little children scampering around and adults idling outside, waiting until sleep and dreams of whatever it was they wanted and might never have would end this ghostly night; and Jessie passed, watching, the wind slapping his big shirt against him, stopping sometimes to open his arms and feel the wind all over. He passed them all, so like them, waiting for sleep, dreading it, not wanting this night to end with its mad winds and endless possibilities, its perfect peace, its oppressive grandeur under which small creatures idled and played.

He walked. And he thought of the song, so beautiful, and the chord change on the chorus that made you ache, that song about the stars. He walked that night with that glorious song, the heat against his skin, a dream of forever being like this, and praying that in his short forever he, just once, would spread himself as warmly and thickly as that wind, or like Weill, let some, for a little while, walk amongst the stars.

Now I've been walking
All the night and day
'Til my eyes grow weary
And my hair turns gray.

And sometimes I think
Maybe God's gone away.
Forgetting the promise
We heard him say.

And we're lost out here in the stars.

Little stars…
Big stars…
Glowing through the night.

And we're lost out here in the stars.

Chapter VIII

I LOVE YOU MORE THAN YOU LOVE ME

The house was empty for some reason, and dark, which it rarely was. Jessie had been upstairs in his room, and had come down to find his mother sitting in the den on a kitchen chair, despite the fact that the den was full of den chairs, and in the dark except for one small, insufficient lamp. She sat crying.

"What's the matter, Mommy?"

She touched his face, and looked at him, studied him, and then took him in her arms and held him close to her. Her warm tears touched his skin. She held him so tightly she scared him. This this overwhelming need was not like her—always so composed, or angry, or kind, but never needy.

"Sit here," she said, and placed him on her lap. He was eleven years old and heavy now. He didn't want to hurt her, but she didn't seem to mind.

"I'm going to tell you something now and you can't tell anyone about it. Okay?"

"Okay."

"You know I love you."

"I love you, too." He held her tighter and placed

his head on her shoulder. He grew more scared. She was strange. He never knew who she would be. Her disapproval could slice like knives she would slash into him without mercy. He would have gladly walked through fire to avoid her disapproval. He could die from that. When he was little and couldn't yet write, he sat next to her and watched her lovely cursive bloom on the white paper like gorgeous flowers, and with paper and pen of his own, he mimicked those long, lovely lines, and when he made one of the letters, the little pretty petals, he beamed, and she would smile. He lived for that, to make her smile for him. He and his father had dismissed one another years ago. When he was five, his father beat him with a belt, yelling, "What's the matter with you, boy. I'm your daddy. You supposed to love me like I'm your daddy." Jessie just lay on the floor curled in a little ball, crying from the pain of the leather stinging his arms and legs and wondering what he had done to make this man hate him so. Jessie avoided him, never got in his way and stayed out of trouble and didn't know what more he wanted because God knew he had nothing else to give.

Talia and Janice treated him like a toy. They used to tell him he was adopted. He looked nothing like them as a child, with his almond eyes and yellowish skin. They told him that their parents picked him up from a doorstep on one of their travels. Day and night they told him this, and he asked his parents to make them stop. His father grinned that lewd grin, with his tongue peeking between his lips and said, "That's right, that's how we found you," and Lulene pursed her lips dismissively, as if he were a fool for listening, and said nothing.

There had been a TV horror show he, Talia, and Janice would watch when the family was stationed in Germany. It terrified him. One night his parents had gone out. They lived in a huge Army apartment complex comprised of several large buildings which faced one another, each apartment with a balcony. Jessie had a terror of thunder and lighting. After watching the show, their parents away, thunder boomed outside and lightning crackled. The girls took him out on the balcony to watch. They'd prove there was nothing to fear, they said. Holding onto them, he followed them out.

"See . . . it won't hurt you," Janice said. Then she pushed him to the ground, and giggling, she and Talia ran through the sliding glass door and locked it behind them, leaving him out there, with the thunder growling and the lightning flashing. He knew that he would die out there. Through the glass, he saw them laughing. With all the power in him he screamed in terror and rage at those smiling faces. He screamed from every nerve in his body, trembling and crying and barely able to stand from fright.

From another apartment in the complex, his parents heard the screaming and returned. They punished him for the embarrassment he had caused them. They berated him for being such a baby. He could only stand there, humiliated, and stare at his sisters and hate them, and at his father, and know him to be vicious; and at his mother, and know that he had been wrong.

Lulene and Grandier were the standard bearers of the race in that community, him being a black officer. Both of them, having been raised as they had, lived in utter terror of giving these white people a reason to dismiss them—to call, or even think them, niggers. A spectacle had been made, and it was his doing, and he would be punished. He could not do what other little boys did. He could not run about without his shirt or shoes. He thought it was the family way until he realized they had to live in constant fear of the finger-on-the-trigger white minds all around them. How many times at how young an age did Grandier tell him that he had to be better than they, brighter, quicker, better dressed, better groomed, just to be considered their equals. Lulene would have them treat her as she had always been treated, as royalty, and her perfectly mannered and perfectly groomed children would be testaments to her own perfection. She was all he had, and Jessie knew that he had to please her to live.

He earned Grandier's wrath and her disapproval with his youthful habit of telling anyone—neighbors, teachers, friends, anyone who would listen—of what had happened in the house, of every detail of any fight or altercation.

"What goes on in this house ain't nobody's business," Grandier told him. His sisters mimicked the line, already terrified of other people's judgments. Lulene would sing him choruses of a popular song called "You Talk Too Much." For her, he learned to hold his tongue, to say nothing to anyone, to keep everything inside, where it belonged. For her.

For her he got straight A's in Catholic schools, where to answer incorrectly got you beaten, nuns lining up the children who had failed, and twisting their ears until the children grimaced in pain and the ears turned beet red, or making them kneel before the class to be beaten with a yardstick.

He lived in terror, the only respite from which, the only thing that made it all worthwhile, being for Lulene to smile down on him, for her to take him and hold him and tickle him, and say, "I love you more than you love me," to which he replied, "No. I love *you* more than you love *me*."

Later, it didn't bother him that she didn't stop the beatings. It only mattered that afterwards, she tended the wounds. When Grandier bought himself a simple round barbecue grill, and Jessie, toying with it, unscrewed the handle, Grandier took off his belt and beat him until his whole body glittered with red welts, some bleeding, and then Lulene took him, and washed him and he thought it was worth it. The stinging all over his body was the price to pay for a moment like this. For kindness, there first had to be blood.

That night . . . that night that changed everything, the smell of the air around them, everything. . . that night he followed her without question. He had heard nothing, and only later learned that Grandier had been drunk, and with a drunk friend who'd boasted that his wife turned over her paycheck to him to do with as he pleased. Grandier then called Lulene, and demanded she do the same. When she refused, he beat her and insisted he would beat her until she obeyed him. The chaos and screaming woke Talia and Janice, who tried to pull Grandier off of her. He threw them across the room and that's when the drunk friend held him. Lulene woke Jessie and told him to follow, which he did, in his night clothes, not knowing why or where they'd go, hurrying behind her, out to the car with Talia and Janice, Grandier drunk and screaming, "Those are *my* kids. You not gonna take my kids outta here. I'll kill you." He threatened to get his gun. He followed them outside, yelling and screaming that he would kill them all, waking neighbors who stood outside to watch. Lulene started the car as Grandier ran toward it, and she locked the doors as he pounded on it, still screaming that they would all die for this, his eyes red and bloodshot, as they so often were now, slurring his words, his tongue swollen and too big for his mouth from the liquor. He jumped on the hood of the car, and Jessie thought that this was their chance, that she should kill him now, and free them; that she should simply run him over and make him die.

Lulene took them to a friend's house, where they stayed for a week or so. They couldn't keep the secret any longer. There was no use hiding now, and Jessie felt relieved. He could say it now. He could tell these people that Grandier was no father, that he beat him and screamed at him and that Jessie hated him. It was finally out in the open, and Jessie spoke freely because he knew that a line had been crossed and they would never go back. Her excuses wouldn't work anymore, that the kids needed a father, that she couldn't support them on her own. Now she had no choice.

Jessie'd spent his life avoiding Grandier's fist, and primping and clowning like a small, talentless vaudevillian to please Lulene. And he was tired. In the fourth grade, he had filled the back of one of his school papers, from top to bottom, every bit of that white paper, with the words, "I hate myself. I hate myself. I hate myself. I hate myself" again and again as if he had gone mad and this mantra had become his world. The nun had offered soothing words as he begged her, with tears in his eyes, not to tell his parents, because he would be beaten for having embarrassed them, for having exposed the forbidden spectacle of their intensely private hell to which they clung so tightly their fingers bled and the shielding of which was worth the suffering.

Jessie knew, finally, that it would have to end.

But it didn't. She went back. After the tears and the drama and the unspoken yet distinct promise of deliverance, she took them back. And Jessie had to face Grandier, face up to the words he had spoken when he thought he was free, and that wasn't fair. He would have rather been beaten within an inch of his life than endure Grandier's wounded stance, his maudlin self-pity and pantomime of pain.

"I wanna talk to you, Son." He used the word "Son" on such occasions, liking its weight, its air of blood connection and blood dominance. "It hurt me what you said to those folks."

He wanted to lie, to say he hadn't said it and be done with it. This wasn't fair.

"You tol' them that I'd never been a real father to you, that you tried to avoid me. Did you say that?"

It wasn't fair.

"Tell the truth, now."

"I told them that I didn't feel close to you," he said.

Grandier lowered his head and shook it slowly from side to side. "That hurts me, Son."

Lies, Jessie thought. He's not human. He can't be hurt. A giver of pain, that's all he is. A monster. The features on his face had come to seem inhuman. The feel of his skin was inhuman. The touch of his lips on Jessie's face made him cringe, as if touched by something evil.

"I'll do better, Son," he said. "And you too. It's not all my fault. You have to talk to me. You never come to me wantin' to do things . . . father-son things . . . Ain't a boy in the world don' wanna go fishin' with his daddy, to go to a game."

"Okay," he said. Grandier embraced him.

Some things did change. Grandier was stationed in another state, but the rest of them remained in Maryland. They told Jessie nothing of it, but some arrangement had been made, some deal was struck between Lulene and her husband whereby he would go away, return at times—for weekends or holidays—but in fact, be banished from that house.

Jessie overheard whispers of divorce. Lulene would discuss it with Janice and Talia, often with tears, and he wondered why she cried when she should be singing and shouting for joy. He asked Talia why she cried.

"Because she loves him," she said.

Those words baffled him, and he watched Lulene, sitting on the piano bench, a friend's arm around her shoulder as she cried and cried, deep tears, and he couldn't imagine that she cried for the love of that man.

Soon after the tears, with Grandier out of sight, she was full of plans, and with her plans and her freedom, she seemed happy. Jessie was happy for her. A schoolteacher all her life, she would go to graduate school, she decided. She bought herself new clothes and fixed things up around the house. She went through the basement and threw out years of accumulated junk they'd carted from place to place.

Doing that, sitting cross-legged on the floor, she came across a box full of pictures. They were portraits of Grandier in his uniform. He had hundreds of them, in all of which he looked severe and military with his insignia blaring. She studied them for a while, and then took a handful, and ripped, and then continued, taking another handful, and using all her strength, grimacing with the effort of shredding the thick stack.

Jessie watched her.

✳✳✳✳✳

The house was empty for some reason, and dark, which it rarely was. Jessie'd been upstairs in his room, and had come down to find his mother sitting in the den on a kitchen chair, despite the fact that the den was full of den chairs, and in the dark except for one small, insufficient lamp.

"I won't be with you as long as I want," she said. "I can't. So you're going to have to be strong for me."

He squirmed to jump from her lap but she held him. "Sometimes I've been hard on you," she said, "and made you do things on your own, but that was because I knew I wouldn't always be here to make it easier, so you had to be hard. You will be alone soon, and I am so sorry."

He looked at her face and couldn't believe what he saw there. He believed her. So he cried. Her sister Shanice always harangued like a demented sage on what would be her early demise, but they all knew she would dance on God's grave. This wasn't like that.

"You have to understand," she said. "I would be here if I could."

"Please don't say that." Tears overwhelmed him. His body heaved and trembled. He touched her. He touched her face, and her hair. It didn't happen like this. He couldn't touch these now and know they'd be taken from him. That would just be too much. All the rest, fine, okay, he was used to it, but not this.

He put his hand against her face. The whole thing only covered her cheek. She looked right at him, and he could barely breathe trying to choke back the tears, the kind that didn't make you yell and holler, but the kind that came from right inside, hopelessly, as if your body bled something precious that it hated to give up and you'd never get back again.

"I know you and your father don't get along, but you're gonna do what you can. He tries his best. He doesn't know. No one knows, except you. I was hard on you 'cause you have to make it on your own. Your sisters have each other, and they're older. There won't be anyone there for you, so I made you hard."

Had she not done her job so well, he would have run screaming. He would have run and screamed and fallen to the ground, his face drenched in what might as well have been acid but he had learned to call tears. He begged her to let him go. Had she gone mad? Or had she finally, like she had longed to do since she first set foot in that Catholic church nearly twenty years ago, had she finally talked with God and been told what she wanted to hear?

"I love you so much," she said, tears in her eyes.

She held him close while small convulsions shook him, his breath snatched up in gulps, gasps, when the heaving allowed. She held him close.

And so he found her in tears in a kitchen chair she had moved to the den, and he sat on her lap, and she told him through her tears that she loved him, and that she would leave him, and in the dark, as if she couldn't let this life go and would drag some precious part of him with her, she cursed him to a life of solitude and missing her.

She sent him to his bed vowing they'd never speak of it again. The next and every subsequent day came and went as if it hadn't happened.

PART II

I know you. I grew up next door to you. You pinched my cheek when I was young and told me I was cute and well-behaved. I played games with your children.

I know you.

I learned my lessons in your schools. There, given your books to read, your novels and your histories, I took them to my room with me when I was lonely. I have read your sonnets, and their austere beauty has swayed me. I've met your Keats and your Yeats. They taught me lessons and kept me company.

The pulse and measured convolution of your fugues I've swayed to. I admit to finding your romantic harmonies self-indulgent, but your progressive and your ethnic ones exploded in my ears like confetti-filled balloons, each brightly colored paper shard bearing tiny flecks of the dirt on your hands and the mud that had been trod beneath your feet, each of which I eyed and studied.

Your God convinced my mother's imagination when I was very, very young and she, in turn, introduced me to His vagaries and ceremonies, His notion, through His Book and the teachings of His minions, that man was created in

His image and stands supreme among His creations, that he, man, holds special place in His heart and scheme.

All of this I know.

But the blood in my veins is not that of those who wrote the books and carved the sonnets and played the harmonies and imagined the God. The blood in my veins, for thousands of years, soaked dirt that you will never walk upon. You will never hear the voices that whisper to me. You will never hear the words that have moved me. Most weren't written. They came from old women and men who had already lived most of their lives. They told me what their years had taught, what horrors they'd seen, or committed, and if they'd managed to do something right. You will never hear the bitterness and honey of those voices, the feel of them, the sighs within them, the laughter, each comma like a shrug of the shoulders, the last words like a stooped back turning away, like old footsteps walking down a road you're just too scared to travel yet, but others walk with dignity. You can't hear them.

There are melodies that take me to tears, the depths of which you cannot know. To you, they might sound light or airy. To you, not grave enough. You will never hear the voices in the horns and see the parade of faces each conjures, black men and women with lives which were neither tragic nor grand but who lived them anyway and made them more than either. A slow dance. Can you dance? Without drinks, or shame, but because the music is so sad you could die to it and it's the only way, at that cheerless moment, to tell him that you love him? Can you? Can you dance?

You will not know what it's like to carry Gods inside you and to heed those outside yourselves. You will never see the ghosts and feel the fates' weight on you, you trying to outrun the past while it effortlessly passes you by, laughing. You will never cry when you think of people like yourself in chains and killed and maimed by lighter men and you won't want vengeance so badly that you taste the blood running down your throat. You will never admit that the four winds are greater than you, and you will die or destroy yourselves trying to subdue them. You will never obey your God because you created him to do your bidding. And you will never know me, who can see you so clearly, and know you so well because you kidnapped me when I was so young and I had to gnaw through my own mind like a fox in a trap does its paw to be free of you. My God, you will never hear the sounds I hear or feel the spirits I feel. You can't know why that E flat wail should say so much you might explode and you will never, never, with tears in your eyes, lay your head on his shoulder, and dance.

Chapter IX

THE LITTLE RED SCHOOLHOUSE

His high school guidance counselor first suggested it. The place was an abstraction to Jessie, like Xanadu or Hades. He couldn't picture himself of it. As black, the place wasn't part of his realm. It was one of the unspoken "can't haves" of his existence, passed down from generation to generation, like a birth defect. Him? At Harvard? It simply would not have occurred. Obviously no family members had attended, nor had any personal friends. When this kindly, portly man suggested he apply to Ivy League schools, a double door opened, a bright light shining from the other side.

A couple of years previous, Talia had left for college—a small, mildly prestigious New York institution—where she would major in art. Jessie and Grandier drove her up there. She cried when they left her in the bare dorm room. Jessie thought she was nuts. He relished the thought of his freedom, plus, displays of emotion made him . . . uncomfortable.

Janice was then a senior at a local black college, where students marched up and down DC streets chanting, "Heathens got a God complex"—heathens being white people. She acquired a black accent and viciously attacked both Jessie and Talia for being too "white." In the mostly white public high school from which both sisters had graduated (and which Jessie now attended) Talia had been a cheerleader, and Janice a student council politico. Talia cried when the team lost big games, causing Jessie hours of Saturday mirth, and had been part of the homecoming court, a ritualistic procedure performed in a dress of volcanic ugliness, the whole of which seemed so arcane and foreign to Jessie it might as well have ended with feasting on human flesh. Both girls had cried to Lulene about boys, white ones, some of whom said they liked them, honest, but just couldn't date them. Jessie avoided such pains by having no high school stake in anything or anyone—save his Family friends. He went because he had to, did as little as necessary, bothered no one, and expected the favor to be returned.

Since Lulene's death, Grandier had grown fatter and meaner. He screamed at Janice for not taking care of the house and her siblings. He'd kept this rural fieldhand mentality wherein the girls assumed maternal duties when the mother died; slopped the hogs, drew the menfolks' baths; but they were neither field hands nor farm folk. He had raised middle-class kids, but his thinking still waded in the bog rural cowtown poverty that had spawned him.

He'd sit in the den, a scotch in his hand, his face puffy, his tongue thick and eyes red while Jessie, Janice and Talia stood in the kitchen, out of his sight, making faces and giving fingers while he stared at the TV and screamed at them. He lived in front of the television, regarding Jessie ignorant for his failure to shout aloud in anticipation of the next shocking plot point. "That says you're smart, when you try to guess what's gonna happen."

The house wasn't clean enough, the meals weren't regular enough, his life wasn't comfortable enough. Janice talked back. Jessie suggested she stop goading him so he would stop, but she couldn't. Her hatred of him grew so big and shrill it was like a banshee living inside her.

"It'd kill your mother to see this house." That was Grandier's favorite line, that "it" would kill Lulene.

"I'm in school," Janice raved, "I have things to do, I am barely here. If you want the house cleaner, get a maid."

"I shouldn't have to get no maid," he replied. "With two great big ol' girls livin' right up in this house."

Janice got revenge. She ate. She ate too much, and she ate in his face and he hated it. He hated a daughter of his fat. His obsession with her weight seemed lurid, as if she had to remain pretty and desirable—for him.

"Girl, you fat as a pig," he would say.

"Daddeeeee," Talia whined in her sister's defense. They had always called him "Daddy." Jessie refused. He couldn't stand the word. With Family members—John and Sally and Emily and Archie—he called him "The Colonel." They picked it up, and everyone called him that, "The Colonel." Jessie searched for, and found ways never to utter "Daddy." Grandier thought "The Colonel" was a term of respect. He bragged to all his friends about how "my boy call me 'The Colonel.'" That rank was one thing he had to be proud of, and he assumed everyone else felt the same.

At school, they'd addressed mailers home, notes about the PTA or something. As a game, the kids put gag names on the envelopes. Jessie wrote "Super Chicken" on his. When the letter arrived, Grandier brandished it at Jessie and challenged, "You write this?"

"Yeah," he replied, quizzical.

Grandier backhanded him across the mouth.

He never forgot the expression on Grandier's face. The bravado masked surprise. Grandier hadn't planned this hit, it had just happened, probably so fast he didn't even have a chance to enjoy it. It had been automatic, and borne of hurt, and both the hurt and the reaction had surprised even Grandier, who turned back toward the television, staring blankly at it, his jaw tensed.

Beatings generally began with a question, and eventually, they became a game, Grandier's goal to humiliate, and Jessie's, requital.

"Jessie . . .?" Grandier called, a voice muffled by the long flight of stairs that always separated them if they were in the house together.

"Yeah?" he answered. A silence followed, and Jessie went about his business.

"Boy, you hear me callin' you?"

"I answered you. You didn't say anything," Jessie yelled back through the empty house.

"When I call you, you get your butt down here."

Jessie found him in the basement, by the steps, near a toolbox.

"What did I tell you about puttin' things back?"

"What?"

"Lookahere."

Grandier pointed to a hammer that lay next to, not in, the toolbox.

"You put that there?"

"Yes. I forgot to put in back in the box."

Jessie bent, picked up the hammer and laid it gingerly in the box.

"What does it take to get through to you boy?"

"It's back now. I didn't hurt the hammer."

Grandier slapped him. "It's not about hurtin' the hammer. It's about doin' what I tell you."

"Okay. I did it. It's back now."

Grandier slapped him again. Jessie stared him straight in the eyes. All his life his eyes betrayed him, said what his mouth wouldn't or couldn't. They stood staring at each other, and when Grandier couldn't stand the screaming hatred in those eyes, he slapped him again, harder this time. Jessie knew he couldn't flinch, and for God's sake he couldn't cry, even with his face on fire. He stared and stared until Grandier felt his own son's hatred like a rapist's touch, and when he did, Grandier clinched his teeth, fury in his eyes, and threw back his fist. It came in slow motion, giving him time to anticipate it, to imagine how the fist would feel when it crashed into his face, to think about the second or two it would take for the pain to sink in, and maybe the thick salt taste of blood in his mouth.

It only dazed him for a second. He didn't fall. He teetered. Trying to keep upright he danced up and down on one foot until the shock passed and he retrieved his balance. He felt his heartbeat in the side of his face so strongly the organ itself might have sat in his mouth. Throughout, though, he still glared his hatred at Grandier.

Grandier had always called him crazy. The boy had been a mystery and an aberration to him since its birth, and now, it stood staring at him like he wanted him to burst into flames so he could hang around to smell the flesh burn. Grandier, finally sick of years of those eyes, turned and walked away. It was the last time he touched Jessie in anger. He knew the boy would never love him.

*****

Jessie passed his time with Family members. They didn't know what went on inside his house. They knew only that Jessie hated Grandier, and Grandier didn't seem to care for him, and that they avoided each other successfully. Even with Lulene dead, even with these closest to him, he didn't talk about it, and not from any active desire to keep a secret, but because he had convinced himself that it wasn't important. Every now and then, the Family stumbled onto details, like the night they made coq au vin at John's house.

The Murphys were poor compared to the rest of them. Their house seemed too small to hold six kids, John being the oldest. It was a family of Irish comedians, all cramped into this small, chaotic, three-bedroom house that was always filthy. Jessie never went in John's room. At first, John wouldn't let him, and after one too many terror-tales of dinnerware oozing with mold growths, Jessie didn't want to.

In the rest of the house, papers, newspapers, and boxes lay piled everywhere. The dining room table was covered with envelopes and loose papers, bills paid, unpaid, dust and dirty clothes everywhere, and in the kitchen . . . each pot was blackened with layers of grease that sandblasting wouldn't dent, ditto the walls, and a couple of roaches always ran for cover when you moved something. The coq au vin was delicious, however, and after they'd eaten the chicken and drunk the wine, Sally drove Jessie home. With her at his side, he put his key in his front door. "Something smells funny," she said. He opened the door and huge black clouds charged outside.

"I think something's burning," Sally deduced.

In the den lay The Colonel, sprawled on the sofa, mouth open, snoring loudly, scotch bottle on the table, the TV blaring, glass in hand, gut rising and falling and his left hand stuck firmly down the front of his pants. On the kitchen stove sat a burning pot bathed in bright flames and spewing smoke like a bellows.

"Wow," exclaimed Sally.

Jessie groped through the thick smoke, filled a pot with water, shielding his face from the heat, thinking a spotted Dalmatian should bark in the distance. Through it all he heard the donkey-like in and out of Grandier's wretched snores, the inhalation like the tearing of limbs, and the exhale like a pervert's sigh.

"You want me to call the fire department?" Sally asked as he battled the flames. "Where's the phone?"

She looked around.

"The phone's under him," she said, nonplussed. "What do I do? I don't wanna wake him up."

And through it all, the man didn't budge. Jessie considered letting it burn, but the benefits of Grandier's death by fire did not outweigh the potential disadvantages. Plus, there would have been a witness.

"Wow," she repeated. "I'm impressed."

*****

He did not attend his high school graduation. In fact, he left school one month early. He set a note in front of Grandier, which he signed without reading, as usual. The note said that a family trip abroad demanded him immediately.

"Don't you know that this is gonna be one o' the bigges' days in your life? And you gonna miss it?" Grandier explained on learning that Jessie would not attend the ceremony.

"It'll be a pretty pathetic life," he replied, "if graduation from Northwood High School is one of its highlights."

"Boy . . ." Grandier replied with sincere sadness. "I jus' don't understand you."

*

Scoring well on his SAT's, Jessie soon had a laundry basket full of college solicitations. However, that guidance counselor's seed had taken root. He would attend an Ivy League, and not one of those tacky ones. Columbia could pass, but Brown and Cornell would never do. He had plans, you see . . .

He was royally pissed that Harvard's first acceptance notice came from the Black Students Association, inviting him, as black, to attend a pre-orientation, presumably to teach him to eat with utensils and not swing from tree branches. He would rather have been struck blind than attend. After all the trepidation, the anticipation, the procrastination, to have it come to this—an unimpressive letter on cheap white bond. He'd given that application special attention. The essay was of particular note. Granted, he sent the same to Princeton, but reading about their physical education requirement, he knew he wouldn't go there. Harvard seemed just right. It sounded like a, "you pay the money, you do what you want" proposition, and Jessie liked that. Harvard showed none of that quasi-parental, "we know what's good for you, young man" Princetonian bullshit. Yale wanted two essays—one too many—so Jessie didn't apply. Of course, Princeton accepted him first, so he had to wait around to see if he would get into Harvard, or be forced to suffer a P.E. class.

He didn't fully believe it. He couldn't be sure (he could not assume the Black Student's Association spoke definitively for the University), not until the next day when the official letter came on the fancy letterhead, crest and all. He was glad he got in, but these folks were on a roll. He hadn't even darkened their door and they had already pissed him off.

*

In case you hadn't noticed, somewhere along the line, between the vicious, whip-wielding nuns, and Grandier's military fist, Jessie had developed an aversion to authority, being told what to do, and having others' assumptions thrust upon him. It started toward the fifth grade. He attended the same grade school for the second year in a row, and a girl who sat beside him, a prim thing with baby-fat, puffed-sleeved dresses and spectacles, turned to him and said, "You used to be such a nice person. What happened?" He beamed.

Right before he fell in with the Family, Jessie took to wearing outrageous clothes—sash belts with feet-long fringes, military surplus coats which scraped the ground, bright orange skullcaps in the heat of summer. In an incident he would remember, one of the few times Lulene didn't cure with bitters and encourage with spurs, she took him aside and spoke sweetly, telling him that he needn't wear such things to pre-empt the world and tell it he rejected its judgment on who he was and how he thought. She said he would easily prove the value of both without props. She gently touched his face, kissed him, and sent him on his way.

She talked him down from that bit of excess, but the root cause remained and intensified in that Hobbesian hotbox called junior high.

*

In ninth grade, they loathed their science teacher Mr. Hoover. He'd spent his life teaching machine shop or something and got stuck teaching science (about which he knew nothing) to mark time until he retired. He spent every class period reading from a science text, and expected not only rapt attention, but, it seemed, gratitude and respect for doing so. He got neither. Students took turns bringing newspapers and reading them openly, each, in turn, sending Hoover into a rage in which his face turned beet red and he stormed to the student, screaming, jowls flapping and pot belly bouncing. He grabbed the student by the neck and gruffly hauled him to the door. If you dared ask a question, he replied with, "If you jus' shut up an' listen, I'll get to it," finally banning questions outright, and continuing his droning recitation. In his Dickensian manner, he intensely loathed each one of them, and in return, they hated him with a fullness that in their youth they had, until then, reserved for relatives.

A hand flew up. They knew it meant trouble. It was John. Family.

Looking over his glasses and seeing John's hand jutting out amidst the perfect rows of immobile, glassy-eyed heads, Hoover read on, trying to ignore it. The hand remained. John propped his other hand under it for support when the shoulder began to ache. Finally, Hoover slapped the book shut and slammed it on the table.

"WHAT IS IT!?" he screamed.

In a studied, respectful, and thoroughly constructive voice, John said, "Mr. Hoover, since we can all read, can't you just assign the chapters and let us read them at home? If you don't want to do anything during classtime, just make it a study hall. We'll do our homework from other classes."

A small chorus of "yeahs" and "why nots" filled the room.

Hoover leaned his arm on the table in front of him and scanned the room, pink flesh dripping over the collar of his threadbare white shirt, his T-shirt visible underneath, the little tie so old it shimmered from too many ironings.

"You think you're real smart don't you?" He paused

and looked at the seating chart on his desk despite the fact he had taught this class for six months.

"John," John prompted.

"A real smartass, aren't you?"

John smiled and shook his head in disbelief.

"AREN'T YOU!" Hoover screamed.

"He's completely nuts," the ever-rational John said, almost to himself, as if just realizing he faced a form of life upon which reason had no impact.

"A smartass," he repeated. "Right?"

"I," John began, having had enough, "prefer the term 'wiseacre'."

Hoover's face turned red in a flash and he bolted down from behind his desk as fast as his stubby little legs could carry him, his head and jowls shaking with fury.

John rose before Hoover got close. "I'm leavin' I'm leavin," he said.

Hoover still charged toward him.

"I'm going. Whaddayawant?"

Hoover ran to him and put his hand on John's neck in his patented manner. John flung the hand from him, turned and glared.

"Don't *touch* me," he said.

The room hushed. He and Hoover stared at one another.

John then turned and walked toward the door.

"Go on! Get outta here!" Hoover yelled after him, walking one step behind.

"Just keep your hands offa me."

Hoover slammed the door behind John, and returned to his raised platform. He placed his glasses on his nose, opened his book . . . and then . . . and then, yes, then continued reading to the class.

Having endured this for one solid year, and, sadly, not having the guts to directly confront him (though in John's case it was less guts and more a naive overestimation of the base intellect of human beings, a topic on which Jessie held no illusions whatsoever), having endured this, they plotted revenge. Jessie had seen one of those '60s-style posters—this one showing a vacuum and the huge legend "HOOVER SUCKS" (in reference to J. Edgar).

That would do nicely.

On the last day of class, before Hoover made his usual entrance, text in hand, Jessie hung the poster on the always-empty blackboard behind Hoover's desk.

They waited.

Hoover walked grumbling to himself and marched straight to his desk, opened the book, and without even as much as a glance anywhere, began reading.

They all sat dumbfounded. They began to titter as he sat up there reading with the words HOOVER SUCKS over his head like an authorial intrusion. As the chuckles grew louder, Hoover glanced upward and paused, waiting for quiet to descend before he read more. Finally, the titters and the murmurs became too much and he slammed his book on the table and angrily scanned the room for a culprit. Before him sat a sea of faces—strangers, small things, enemies—laughing, the titters ballooning into outright guffaws, gut wrenching, tear stained gales of fall-outta-your-chair har-dee-har-hars, some clutching their middles and pointing their skinny little fingers at him. His head shook, the blood rose, turning even the top of his shiny head a shade of rose. He swung around. The strings let out a stinging sound as in old film previews and looming above him, accusatory, like Uncle Sam's finger at the melodrama's traitor . . . the words:

HOOVER SUCKS

He trembled. It started in his feet, a murmur, vibrations, as if he were a rocket preparing for launch, missing only the tangle of wires and metal, the disembodied countdown and billows of white smoke against the bright blue sky. It traveled up his limbs, his legs, his pelvis and torso, the fingers started wiggling, the arms themselves then trembled and finally the head, as if ready to shoot off his neck like a bespectacled, pudgy bomb.

"Little PRICKS!" he bellowed.

Those who hadn't yet dissolved into fits of laughter, now did so. Whistles and hoots flew. Spitballs and paper-wads launched toward him in a feathery parody of warlike bombardment. A rhythm grew—feet stamping, hands clapping—and the primal chant, "HOOVER SUCKS, HOOVER SUCKS, HOOVER SUCKS . . ."

It was glorious.

"GET THE HELL OUTTA HERE, ALL O' YA!"

The chants and claps and paper wads flew as they rose, hooting and hollering, stamping militarily to "Hoover sucks" while Hoover screamed, holding the door like a stark raving butler, waving his arm toward the other side as if furiously banishing a lingering fart.

"I never wanna see yer ugly faces again! Go on. GET OUT! GET OUT!!"

The sound faded as they marched down the empty, locker-lined hallway, the first ones out of class. Their voices and footfalls echoed softly off the tiles and linoleum, and from a distance, still, that diminishing figure, that angry voice that didn't matter at all anymore.

All four legs stiffened and twitched uncontrollably as Caesar lay on his side. Jessie could only see one of the dog's eyes but that was filled with terror and you could tell some of the twitching was him trying to stand, to overcome what his body was doing. Jessie had seen it happen a couple of times in the past few months. Both times, he'd petted Caesar and stayed with him and it had passed in moments. Maybe a muscle spasm. Jessie hadn't thought much of it.

As he he grew older, with Lulene gone and him in the house with Grandier and Janice and Corinne away at school, the dog meant less and less. The thing he had once dearly loved became a burden. Something to clean up after and feed. It didn't seem to belong any more. It was a thing of childhood that he no longer wanted. He resented the obligation, implied by its very presence, its existence, to love it. He'd get angry, and yell at it if it pissed on the floor in the basement, even if he did so only because Jessie wouldn't take him out. Couldn't it see it belonged to a time when he was small and weak and needed its comforts? He'd outgrown those things and wished that everything that had to do with them would disappear. Its needs were like pin pricks to him. He couldn't get coats from the closet without rattling the leash which brought him running, tail wagging, tongue hanging, thrilled to be going somewhere. Jessie felt murderous for refusing. He'd yell and shoo it away. Later, he wondered if the dog knew what had happened. He wondered if Caesar had smelled the changes in him the same way it used to smell his loneliness and lay its head beside him. He wondered if he smelled the fury as keenly. The loneliness he had helped cure, but what could he do with fury?

It walked around that silent, mainly empty house full of dead woman's things and a man growing old in front of a glowing TV with a drink in his hand and a boy growing up full of rage and hardness, with nothing there for him except to wander, room to room, idly and lonely, like an inverse ghost, a living thing among the dead.

That night, Jessie was alone. The dog went into convulsions. At first, Jessie thought the spasm would pass like the others. He waited, and watched as that one visible eye stared up at him, saying, "this is your chance at redemption, to make amends for all the cruelties, small and large." The loving eyes, as always, looked to him for something he didn't have to give.

Jessie stared down at that terrified thing as its body flailed against the hard ground. He saw blood on the pavement as its position shifted with the constant violence. Just sixteen, he couldn't yet drive. When he couldn't bear to see those streaks of blood grow anymore, he got on the ground and tried to hold the dog up, away from the rough concrete so that it wouldn't hurt itself, but the spasms wouldn't stop. He cried with frustration. He seethed at Grandier for being away. Most times, he would have paid to make him go. He searched phone directories for veterinarians' phone numbers and got only recordings.

Years later, he remembered the sight of the dog on the pavement, how it dragged itself across concrete and left a trail of its own blood. He remembered phone call after phone call to find a vet who'd come and get him, and then immediately worrying about the cost if someone did. He worried that Grandier would beat him if it cost too much. He remembered going from room to room, window to window, and praying for Grandier's car to drive up. He ran to neighbors as a last resort to beg for near-stranger's help. He finally found one who'd take him to the animal hospital. But most of all, he remembered helplessness. He remembered guilt. The creature pleading for help and spilling its blood while he watched, helpless, penitent. He knew that this ghastly dumbshow was his just punishment.

Jessie didn't leave the car when the neighbor dropped Caesar at the vet. An attendant came and took the dog. Jessie never saw him again. While he lived, sick, trussed up and immobile, Janice went to visit, as did Grandier, who called Jessie heartless for not doing so.

The dog, Caesar, that he had once so loved, was gone.

and we're lost...

out here

in the stars...

Mark died and Chuck got injured in a motorcycle crash. An acquaintance told him one night at a club. He hadn't seen the acquaintance in a long time, and he kept saying "You remember Chuck. You remember Chuck," and offering descriptions. "Oh, you mean the guy . . ." Jessie would say, counter-describing another Chuck or Charles. The acquaintance insisted they had played together, at the bar. Jessie didn't remember. "Well," the acquaintance said, "he's in a veteran's institution. He's practically a vegetable now."

Jessie couldn't remember Chuck, but it struck him that lives around his, like his, were in-progress, rockets steaming on their pads, too late to abort, ready to soar or explode—in full swing, like parties with one too many drunken guests. He had known his own catastrophes, friends had had babies, lost their lovers or their minds. Some sat idle in wheelchairs not knowing where they were. Lives were . . . in progress, like when he saw Mark's name in that bold faced type, Jessie having developed the habit of scanning the obits in the film and TV trade papers, which put him a notch below Grandier's sister, who at least saved that vice for her dotage. First he would read the name, weeding out the females. Then, he scanned for the age, and if they died in their thirties or forties or twenties, he'd read on, a little sense of victory if a car wreck, a long fall, or anything non-AIDS-related caused it. Some days, only old folks died, and he felt grimly relieved, as one would who felt the world lay securely in its orbit. On seeing the names of young men, he steeled himself, like when you pull the scab from a cut. Most died "after a long illness," and were survived by sisters and nieces. To date, they had all been strangers.

He turned the page and that name slapped him. Those bold letters, accusatory, and he almost looked around for the grinning face of the malevolent son of a bitch who had put it there.

Mark had died months ago. The notice said he died of cancer. Mark's was always a silly, proud clan, Mark's mother once scolding to her out-of-work son with, "There's never been a *Dyer* on unemployment." Jessie hadn't talked to him in a year, barely at all since a strained lunch after Jessie had moved into his barrio digs. Mark tried to reassure him by spouting platitudes about everything having a meaning and God not giving you any more than you could handle. Jessie wanted to laugh and ask if he had never heard of suicide. They had barely spoken since. Mark should have told him, though. Silly as it sounds, he should have told Jessie he was dying. That was important.

Thick clouds swirling, churning, haunting
Make me wonder, wishful, taunting
Deep beneath I sense you wanting
Tawdry hopes you find beneath you,
Love and want and broken need

He had boyfriend potential. He did. Really. About 5'8", thin, big ears, big nose, but somehow managing cute, even sexy. Jessie was attracted, yet repulsed. There was something intriguing, but also, bubbling underneath, the possibility of complete madness. Dreadlocks hanging halfway down his back didn't help. What a short white guy was doing in LA with foot and a half dreads, God only knew. He looked like a serial killer.

They finally spoke about a year after first eyeing each other at local bars. His name was Dylan, and he now wore a crewcut. He spoke with the dismissive, "fuck that" braggadocio of the outcast who'd been lucky enough—and it's only luck—to survive, and even flourish, on his own terms, but who would never forgive the slights and hurts he suffered before privilege. He painted, and owned a design business. An artist. His work traveled, sold, and he sometimes answered calls to speak at arts colleges and seminars.

Yes, there were warning signs. He took on a grim air when staring men down, as if he needed something small—not affection or love or anything so grand, but sex—to dominate, submit, whatever. But talking with him, Jessie saw him caring, almost sweet, both of which popped out of him unexpectedly, to him as well, like a twitch he tried to suppress but which snuck up on him anyway.

He admitted being a control freak, but jokingly, or, to Jessie, with such amusing stridency you didn't take it seriously. He had never worked for anyone else. Even way back when he panhandled for food money on San Francisco streets, he refused to work for anyone else. Part of Jessie admired that. Part of him thought, "What an ass," the Mr. Hyde and Dr. Jeckylls of him.

Their first time, Dylan came on too rough, and Jessie put him down, then drew him into something softer. The swipes turned to touches. The bites to kisses. He didn't talk much about himself, and had no interest in Jessie's dissections and descriptions of this or that. He asked no questions. He was equally stingy with responses. He liked getting stoned, and compulsively switched channels on the TV from a bed canopied in gauze in a room stuffed with statues and artifacts from all over the world, man-sized Mexican church Christs and dummies wearing shiny Chinese robes, fans with serpentine designs and trinkets and doodads from the places he'd worked and seen. His was a reeking, mordant chiaroscuro of a place. A lair. An insular world you could see, but could not enter. All you could do was accept it—look in from a personal distance and live temporarily beneath it, as a tourist wouild the rituals of a foreign folk.

Next time they met, Dylan gave himself entirely, and it was soft and slow and bright and laughing. He looked in Jessie's eyes and laughed when they came, when each move wracked their bodies with shudders one-half inch from pain. Jessie thought he had done the impossible and found a man he might love; he thought he finally heard the murky, distant bells. It was their best time.

On their third date, there was little to say. Dylan really tried to do it softly and look him in the eye, but he needed that small thing. Jessie saw the flickerings of contempt in Dylan's eyes, barely perceptible, but there. He still needed dispassion, dispensing at least emotional pain with his pleasure because the ones who tolelrated that would never have power over him. He would revile them too often for that.

He canceled two dates in a row and Jessie never heard from him again. Next time Jessie saw Dylan, he walked with a man whose needs jibed with his wants. After feeling hurt and rejected a moment, Jessie felt cheapened that he had dated someone who wanted so little, foolish for thinking he would learn to want more, silly for hoping to teach him.

There must have been a normal way, a right way. Not the thunderbolts of fiction nor the devastation of loneliness. Was that way closed to him? Was it his past? Was he so different? Did what he loved and thought mean so little to so many?

If you look long enough at a human face, it loses

its grip. Jessie could look at a face on the street or a bus, study it, and let it be random. Those wet and glassy indentations at the top, with folds of flesh above them that slip up and down like an adder's tongue slips in and out of its mouth, and the redder, puffy sets of flesh toward the bottom . . . and these tiny strings that pop right out of the skin, like long lazy blades of grass. If you stared at somethim long enough, stripped it to its bare components, they could be arranged in myriad ways. He feared that few wanted to know that because it makes for endless possibilities, the existence of which might drive most mad, the existence of which may be one definition of the same. Jessie thought someone like Dylan might see the possibilities, and maybe he did, but instead bathing in them, examining them, he built a shelter of cannabis, gauze and statuary and moved himself to the warm, still safety inside. He *had* potential.

Oh well.

I came, I saw, I dreamt to conquer
Haze and darkness made me falter
My fault, yours, it doesn't matter
My fault though, I'm sure

I thought you wanted someone like me
I just wanted what I glimpsed beneath the haze
Behind it, shrouded, closed from view
So close, too far, what I wouldn't do
To put it there, what I had needed
And thought you wanted
Too much to ask. My fault
Should not have been so wrong

"Ask not for whom the bell tolls . . . It's no one you know."

— Overheard, unidentified Harvard student

Chapter X

SUSANNA'S BUTT

It looked like the glossy brochures. That reassured the Colonel. He, with his longtime girlfriend Tina, drove Jessie up to Harvard from Maryland. She was an administrator in the DC government who seemed so coquettishly naive, so cartoonishly bubbleheaded, you expected a short guy in a clown suit to round the corner any minute, stick a horn to her butt and honk it—a cloak, he learned, she wore for men.

The Cambridge streets were winding and narrow and quaint, and enough cobblestone remained to evoke the venerable and antiquated. They drove through the gates of Harvard Yard, and found Wigglesworth Hall, the dorm to which he had been assigned. Wigglesworth. Wigglesworth. Some old rich white man had gone through life called Wigglesworth. Jessie would have pitied him, but ridiculous as it was, the name just sounded so goddamned nauseatingly rich.

On his housing form, Jessie'd requested a single room. He'd offered good reasons for requesting it. He'd lived practically alone for years and had grown accustomed to his peculiar ways. He was a writer, and that required privacy, the proverbial room of one's own. He made it sound quite high-minded and absolute.

He entered the assigned room on the first floor of the old freshman dorm. One bed sat in the living room, and bunkbeds occupied the bedroom. He let it pass. He'd anticipated this, and requested, should a single prove impossible, roommates of like mind and temperament. Involved in the arts. English majors or Visual Studies, folks with whom he would discuss jazz or Orson Welles, Proust, whom he had never read but would pretend he had, or, perhaps, Barth. That might be fun.

Before leaving, Grandier reminded him of the minority mixer that evening . . . yes . . . and said goodbye, added yet another, "I'm proud of you son," and took his leave. Since gaining entrance, he heard little from Grandier save, "My boy's goin' to Harvard." Always "My boy." The possessive, save anyone should minimize the link between the child and himself. It was his achievement that his son should attend the nation's premier University. "That boy's gonna cos' me $15,000 a year," he invariably added, grinning.

"Ooowwweeee!" the friend would say. "Why not jus' sen' him on to Howard. Tha's a good school. How many colored folks they got out there?"

Grandier would looked scornfully at the fool. "I got money. What you mean Howard? This Harvard University. Don't hardly take nobody, black *or* white. But they took my boy." Jessie didn't begrudge him his pride.

Thus he sat alone in his Harvard dorm room, two roommates, two strangers yet to arrive. He set up his stereo as the sun set on Harvard Yard and the black students prepared for their University-sanctioned mixer (he had arrived a bit early and the white folk weren't due 'til the next day), their voices peeking through his first-floor windows, their footfalls audible . . . he set up his stereo, Family members having spent parental cash on identical sound systems, and he played some late fusion, ECM, pastel harmonic stuff, still unfamiliar with the gods he would soon worship. He took the lower bunk in the bedroom, pleased at securing the prime spot, and he listened to the student sounds and conjured images of what the next years would bring and who he would be on the other side. Finally, he slept and dreamt of skyscrapers, snakes, and tunnels.

Next morning he woke to idling car engines and parental chatter. Right outside, the bulk of students hauled duffel bags from station wagons and lugged them into buildings. Watching through the window, Jessie was shocked that many of them knew each other. How? Disappointment also registered. They looked unimpressive, and their parents (could it be?) vulgar.

Hearing his own front door open, annoyance welled up in him. After what he saw outside, he hoped no one would show.

He threw on some clothes and entered the living room to face six: two students, three parents, one sibling—all black.

He played it cool, but he had read the stats. He

knew that tops, ten to twelve percent of that incoming freshman class was black. No more. Not a whiz at mathematics, he still figured the probability of three black frosh coincidentally thrown together to be pert-near zero.

The parents questioned him as if he were going to date their sons instead of ignore them. They looked askance when he mentioned film and English literature. They looked askance at his longish hair, dirty jeans, and Wallabees. Marcus was pre-med and Henry had already planned his political career right down to the sex scandals. Jessie was furious.

EXPLICATION

In his teens, Jessie had developed a Nietzchean worldview, which was impressive, kinda, considering he hadn't heard of Nietzche. There were leaders in this world, and followers. There were those destined to rise above the rabble, and those condemned to wallow in it. Need you ask in which category he placed himself? He saw no reason why those like himself should be shackled by the same constraints as ordinary folk, those who desperately sought guidance and a well trod path to follow, without which they'd be completely lost, like tit-suckling pups whose mothers got shot. In more severe moods, he insisted that exalted ones had the right to kill. There were those who deserved to die. That senator from Alabama or Tennessee, or some such state, he deserved to die—ninety-nine or 190 years old—who'd been shot and had the gall to live. He was one of those who stood on doorsteps beating on blacks with brickbats. He called out dogs and pink-faced cracker sheriffs to beat black people and vowed they would never go to school with *his* kids. Jessie'd watched it on TV when he was young—black people getting bitten by whites' dogs and hosed like pigs by water gusts so strong they ripped the clothes from their backs and knocked them off their feet. He remembered cringing in pain as if it happened to him when he saw a dog held by a filthy white hand tear open a black man's arm. Men like that Alabaman he dreamt of having nerve enough to kill.

Those less horrible he hoped to ignore. Simple people, plain white folk . . . they unnerved him. Madison Avenue images of apple pie and red, white and blue sent chills down his spine, like those that might afflict a Jew on seeing jackboots and goosesteps. Simple people. The average man would have lynched him, or watched it and wanted it, or called him "nigger" or "boy," or tolerated it. All of them stood suspect. How many would have had the strength or vision back in '55 to stand with him, to treat him like a human being. Few. Very few. Even now they made excuses for themselves. "Can't be held to modern standards" when talking of their slaver idols, absolving themselves amidst sin, like priests performing their own wedding vows. When he looked at them, he knew they could not be trusted.

He thought he knew what it took. He'd been with the Family for years, all of them smart, all of whom read books and opened their eyes wide, curious, cringing at nothing, taking no sticky sweet force-fed illusions for the real thing. They would rather have vomited than swallow those.

He expected at least as much from Harvard. He expected to meet a lot of people like Family. He expected them to discuss the books they'd read and the music they'd heard, to wax rhapsodic over bright afternoons in museum sculpture gardens. He wanted to trust them.

He spent his first six months as if in a fog. He said little, and spent most of his time alone. His roommates quickly sickened him. Henry, with his black Poindexter persona and not an ounce of magic in him, pumping hands, running up to strangers and sticking out his pudgy little paw while adjusting his thick glasses saying, "I'm Henry. I saw you in that seminar on buttsucking through the years and I really liked what you had to say about shit not tasting that bad, and I just wanted to meet you." And Marcus who chose doctoring not from a desire to help or heal, but a desire to ensure a hefty income, who had already chosen his house in a first-tier suburb, a nice-sized practice composed of the few area blacks and a healthy dose of whites, taking pride in having strived almost to the top of his preferred ladder.

They thought Jessie was nuts. Early on, they sat around the living room and talked. Marcus and Henry talked about breaking walls down, of getting in and clawing your way up the lily-white ladder to sit proudly as the first black face here or there. Jessie tried to tell them that it didn't work that way. He told them they might get there, but if so, only at the largesse of those who might be their enemies. They might get there, but so belittled and beaten and tired they might as well curl up and die; that no matter where they went to school— they could tattoo the Harvard crest to their butts and moon every sentient being—but to most white men looking on, it would be just another black bottom.

They didn't see it that way. They thought white folks would come around. But Jessie had seen it with his own eyes, through the Colonel, all the bowing and the scraping and perfection; and in private, all the rage and violence . . . it didn't work. If you played by their rules, they won. That's all. That was it. No exceptions. That's why he would make his way with the image or the word. You could maybe win that way. Your mind transposed to paper and print could not be compromised unless by sheer knavery or foolishness. "But they simply won't go or they simply won't read," Marcus and Henry protested. "Perhaps you can play them," Jessie said, like the sax or the xylophone, coax notes from them they didn't mean to make, coax reactions and emotions they didn't mean to show. You had to play them. You could make them scream for more that way.

That's what he learned from his mother. The way she had of being something more than they, of walking as if she were beyond their most fevered dreams, as if the spirits and the gods walked with her and she knew it. Teaching, she always worked in black schools, teaching kindergarten kids their letters, words and numbers because she knew how good she was and knew that such gifts should not be wasted on white ones while black ones went begging. Marcus and Henry were defeated already because in their own eyes, they had to elevate themselves to a white man's level, instead of deigning to suffer them, despite the fact they would never rise to theirs.

They didn't get it.

Slowly, they stopped asking him to black student association functions, seminars on dressing for success, on "networking," and other such things. Soon, their very presence irked him beyond reason. His resentment grew—of the University itself, which not only stacked completely incompatible black people in this one room, but had filled this whole section of the dorm with nothing but black people. The very notion of this place having the nerve and stupidity to assume he couldn't survive in the bulk of their world infuriated him.

Then he heard about the "Psycho Single."

Now, he thought himself the quintessence of "normalcy." His temper was even; immune to both manic highs and distasteful lows. He worked hard at, and generally succeeded in, seeing the truth in persons and situations, rarely falling prey to manipulators, liars, sycophants and flatterers, and, situation permitting, spoke the truth more often than not. He had a plan for his life, one developed at a young age, and maintained, more or less, and worked steadily toward. He wanted something, wanted it more than his life—to be called an artist, and a great one, his "something to live for" this was, and he assumed, knew, that everyone else could and did claim the same, something for which he or she would sacrifice anything, possessions, persons, a limb or two, to get. His aesthetic was brutal. It allowed him nothing. He assumed everything to be the price he would gladly pay for his achievement. He expected little fun, no lovers, few friends, no home, and each attempt toward any of these to end in wrenching tragedy from which he would cull yet another masterwork.

Corners of the world await
But no one there to greet me
Horses bucking wild
Horizons stretched to aching

His enslavement to his art would be complete.

Leaving poems behind me
No one dares to read
You'll be out there somewhere, hurting me

Those he loved would die, or he would have to leave them, tearfully, achingly, like Lassie did in the color shows, leaving him bawling when he was younger. But he would make the hard choices, and he would move on, to endure this life of wandering to which he had been cursed by a weeping woman on a kitchen chair in a darkness of a family den.

You'll be crying. I'll not hear
Soar without you, singing songs
I'll forget you
I'll forget you

~~~~~~~~~~~~

Talia and Janice stared out the den window into the gray outside, waiting for Grandier because they knew that when he came, she would be dead. They planned, this day, to disconnect the life support and let her die. Jessie joined the vigil, but the point was moot by now. He'd given up. He'd prayed and offered up everything he had, short of his life, even that, and forfeited all future favors and rewards if only God would let her live. But he would not. He would not grant that one small wish, and therefore, Jessie thought, was a cheat and a liar and deserved contempt. He sat there with them in silence, for lack of anything else to do, and for fear of being called heartless if he did not. He waited.

Finally, Grandier's big brown car with the white vinyl top pulled into its space outside. Talia and Janice stood up and moved closer to the window. He thought he saw water already in their eyes. He felt none welling in his own.

They waited, motionless, and watched as Grandier walked toward the house, put his key in the door, and entered. Grave, eyes wet and red, air stoic, military, he stood in the doorway to the den and said, "Your mother died today at 12:52." Immediately, Janice and Talia burst into tears. Jessie stared at them in wonder. Janice bolted past Grandier and ran up the steps. Talia
~~~~~~~~~~~~

ran after her. Jessie sat in his chair, wondering how they could have called forth tears after all this time. It seemed like years—of going back and forth to the hospital, of knowing it was hopeless and knowing she would die and he couldn't imagine crying any more. When Grandier and his sister Ruby looked at him, expectant, he ran up the steps as if he, too, had been overcome.

He found Talia and Janice in the latter's room, crying desperately in each other's arms. He sat near them on the bed and tried to cry, but couldn't. Talia broke down about once an hour like clockwork for the next two weeks. Janice, on the other hand, went into less regular, but more violent, spasms of grief throughout the period.

Jessie accompanied Grandier to shop for caskets, the solemn salesman reciting the virtues of one model over the next. "This one is lined with lead, and is guaranteed leak-proof, and can withstand a 20-megaton nuclear blast." Jessie didn't really care if Lulene got wet any more.

"I don't want nothin' but the best," Grandier intoned to the salesman, as if she would have been pleased to know that her corpse would rot in such luxury.

Talia returned from shopping with a powder blue shroud. Mentioning the brand name she said, "Nothing but the best for Mommy." The corpse would rot in the finest of coffins, and look smashing doing it.

Relatives, mostly Grandier's, descended on the house. Neighbors, as if by instinct, baked food and brought it over, glazed expressions on their faces, acting as if they hadn't the faintest idea how the stuff borne on the platter got there, but, hey, since it was ... why don't you take it.

The wake was impressive. Held in a suburban mortuary, lines to march past the casket wound out the door, down the steps, and outside. Who were all these people? Among them, Jessie saw his fourth-grade teacher. He couldn't have imagined a meaningful encounter between Lulene and that woman. There were people there who must have met her only once, but they went out of their way to come here. The mortician wondered at the sheer numbers of them. This impressed Jessie. It justified his thinking her a formidable woman.

Inside the wake room, Grandier, Talia, Janice and Jessie wandered about, the casket against the wall, the mortician instructing the family to stand thusly, so the guests could file past them, greet them, and then pass the coffin. Open or closed? Open or closed? Who wants to look at a corpse, Jessie thought? The very idea seemed barbaric, above and beyond the babararisms that had already taken place, not to mention those still in the planning stages.

A decision would be made. The family would view the body, and decide if the coffin would stand open or be closed. Grandier's sister reminded them, "You don' want people thinkin' she look too bad to see."

Jessie started chuckling. He turned to a window so the family would think he was lost in solemn contemplations. The mortician who was already there couldn't open the casket. He had to summon some specialist in casket openings. He scurried from the room to do so.

"Why don't we just leave it closed," Jessie suggested.

"You don't want people thinkin' there was somethin' wrong wit' her," Grandier's sister repeated.

"Something wrong? With a dying woman? Sacrebleu!" Jessie mumbled.

When the white-gloved casket opener arrived, he hurried and scooted and stage-managed them all into a viewing arc around the coffin. A smile tickled the ends of Jessie's mouth. He battled the twitches. He fought them bravely, but he was no match.

"What's with the gloves," Jessie whispered to Talia.

"Shhsshhh!" she hissed back.

The casket opener turned his back to them and slowly, oh so slowly, lay his white cotton fingers under the waist high rim of the coffin and, in a liquid motion worthy of a prima ballerina, brought both hands up and aloft with such seamlessness and grace you expected plies in accompaniment. He then moved aside. Talia, as soon as the body was revealed, burst into loud fits of weeping. Janice panted and heaved, her hand to her chest, bent over at the waist, water pouring from her eyes before she turned and bolted from the room. Grandier's sister ran after her while Grandier and the white-gloved mortician tended Talia's more demure response. They heard Janice through the closed door. "GET OUT! GET OUT! JUST LEAVE ME ALONE!"

Jessie felt relieved. He had feared he might fall on the floor laughing maniacally and be stoned for witchcraft or locked up for life. He could see the headlines: "the boy who laughed at his own mother's corpse." As it happened, though, the whole thing sidestepped humor, as a cat would a turd in the walkway . . . and fell headfirst into the pit of absurdity.

Talia bawled, and even through two doors Janice wailed, and against the wall in this room lined with chairs sat an extremely expensive coffin in which lay, wrapped in an outrageously costly designer nightgown, as if she were off to seduce death itself, an inanimate sack of painted-up bones with a bad wig that bore as much resemblance to his mother as a dead mule would have laying there so bedecked. How this not-even-ridiculous, this simply unnecessary sight could drive one to tears he couldn't understand. He knew better than to try.

"She was so beautiful," Talia wept. "People shouldn't see her like this."

Grandier wanted the casket open.

"She don't look bad," his sister added.

"Talia, it's not her," Jessie heard himself say. He'd never learned. His reasonable talk had always failed to convince anyone in that family of anything. His, to his mind, impeccable logic held no sway. "It's just an empty sack. Look at it. It doesn't even look like her anymore. Whatever was in it is gone. It doesn't matter what happens to that."

Talia looked at him. Her sniffling quieted somewhat.

It's not what she expected to hear, and she listened.

The casket would remain open.

The mourners filed by, and Jessie and the others stood in a line, Janice having returned from her solitude with only red eyes to show for it and a fixed "I'm fine" smile. They all stood in a line as the mourners filed by and shook each of their hands and offered whispered condolences to each one of them. Most of them didn't bother Jessie. Most of it had no effect on him. It was just pointless, catharsisless ritual, formality in the most Victorian sense, something to be tolerated because one hadn't the power not to.

Over time though, some of them, the ones who really cared—and you could tell—they got to him, and he hated them more than all the others. He imagined all of them waiting for a scene, hysterics and tears, even the nicer ones deep down wanting to feel this gash vicariously, talk themselves into feeling its tingling and sting, as if this were a small town train wreck and the folk had run from all around to see the carnage because it was something, it was hard and sure and bloody and unequivocal and they could find those things nowhere else.

He hated the ones who cared, because they made him want to cry. When they approached with their wounded looks he felt the tears and grief well up in him, and he had to choke them down like the foulest tasting bile. When they whispered in his ear he wanted to vomit grief, but he wouldn't. He wouldn't look them in the eye, and he said nothing for fear his voice would crack or tears would fall. He filled his head with songs. He sang them to himself, pop melodies in his head, over and over so he wouldn't have to hear the pain.

He did not cry.

~~~~~~~~~~~~

The morning was appropriately gray. The days in-between had passed like roaches, scurrying frantically out of sight, into cracks and crevices you didn't know existed. At least this, the funeral, finally, would be the last of it, the end of the whole exhausting business.

The morning was appropriately gray.

Black limousines lined the street. He'd never been inside one before. It surprised him. He didn't expect so much room. No one spoke on the way. He just looked out the window.

The morning was appropriately gray. Many cars attended the gravesite, snaking all the way down the winding roads as far as he could see. They put her in the part of Arlington National Cemetery with individual headstones, not the huge expanses of identical upright slabs with convex tops, seas of them, like fields of hard white wheat that wouldn't move when the wind blew marking the bodies of men who died in wars—
~~~~~~~~~~~~

thousands of them.

The morning was appropriately gray. The previous night's rain had soaked the ground, so the cemetery had placed boards, long wooden boards on which you could walk, a pathway of them from the road to the gravesite. An awning had been erected, and under it, some metal folding chairs. The girls got single white roses to hold, and a large bouquet of red ones adorned the coffin.

The priest spoke some words, and then they all walked away, back across the boards and back to the limousines, outside of which Jessie had to stand, and endure again the sympathy and tears of all these people as they shook his hand or touched his face or kissed him and cried and he had to sing his private little song in his own little head to stop himself from dying.

The morning was appropriately gray as the limousine disgorged them at the house, and upstairs, taking off her special dress Talia said, "I can't believe we just did that."

The morning was appropriately gray, and just as the evisceration on a kitchen chair in a den full of den chairs had been erased, to Jessie, already, it was as if she had never been.

He'd heard about the "psycho singles" in the Harvard freshman dining hall, an immense room with oak walls—floor to twenty-foot ceiling—adorned with six-foot tall portraits of pink-cheeked old white men, long, dark wood tables, and an old enormous chandelier hanging from the middle of ceiling.

"Bonkers," the girl sitting a table over hollered. He was hiding in a corner. He ate at odd times, when the place wasn't crowded, either the very beginning or the very end of the mealtimes. This girl screamed, as if playing to the rafters despite the fact that her audience of two sat right next to her.

"He was some prodigy or something . . . I don't know . . . a tabla virtuoso from Salt Lake City or something . . . I don't know. But he was NUTS."

"What? How?" her audience asked.

"He stank."

Pause.

"So what he stank."

"No," she said, "I mean REALLY stank."

"Are we talking fecal stink here?"

"And more . . ."

She looked to each of her three listeners, building suspense like a master griot.

"They say he missed the toilet."

The male listeners looked to one another.

"Guys miss. So what."

"I'm not talking about pissing."

"Eeuuuggcchhh!?" Cheeks flew upwards and noses down in schoolmarmish distaste.

"They put him in South House. They always say the singles are full but they keep some for the real loons—'Psycho Singles'."

First thing next day Jessie made an appointment with the Dean of Housing, the one who lorded over rooming mishaps and incidents.

He spent that morning getting his Irish up, getting mad. He could do that, talk himself into states, like an actor prepping a role. He wandered around campus practically mumbling in anger and snarling at no one, recounting the litany of injustices endured due to some fool's arrogance and stupidity.

At the appointed time he sat in Dean Hargreaves' outer office. Summoned inside, he was shocked to see a black man behind the Dean's desk. Jessie immediately breathed easier. This would be quicker than he thought.

"I understand you have a problem with your rooming situation," the Dean said, after the usual salutations.

"I'd like to be transferred to a single."

"Is there a clash with your current roommates?"

"No real clash. I'd just prefer a single. I find it

difficult to live with people. I requested one on my housing application, explaining why it would be best for me. Seeing that I had been assigned roommates despite my explicit requests, I decided to give it a try, but it's not working."

"Why not?"

Third degree he didn't need. He'd requested a single. The request had been ignored. He had tried it their way. It hadn't worked. Now, he thought, take defeat up the butt like a man, and give him what he wants.

"I resent the fact," he replied, bristling, "that everything I wrote on the housing application was ignored. I had asked for roommates with like interests, instead I got a future Junior State Assemblyman and an anesthesiologist, some idiot obviously assuming that the fact of being black would outweigh our differences, as if we could always compare notes on looting and ogling white women and amuse ourselves with watermelon-spitting contests."

There was a long pause.

"Uh . . . Actually," he sputtered. "I made those arrangements."

Jessie stared him straight in the eye and took the beat. "Whatever," he flatly replied.

Four days later, he hauled his butt, and his belongings, to South House.

*****

South House (dorms at Harvard are called Houses—Adams House, South House, etc.) had been part of the once all-female Radcliffe campus, and sat approximately half a mile due north of Harvard Yard. In the pre-coed days, the women were locked up there to shield them from those pesky penises. Now it was just a part of the full coed campus, with a reputation as a haven for radical separatist lesbians and suicidals. Assignment thereto was akin to Siberian exile in the eyes of most students—highly undesirable. Jessie loved it.

His single room occupied about 10' x 10' space. The bathroom was down the hall, but the room had a free-standing sink. The missing toilet would have elevated it to full cell-like glory. The previous occupant had painted strange, cacophonous streaks of color, willy-nilly, on one wall. It was obviously the work of a madman. It reminded him of animations he had seen of the manner in which the severely disturbed record visual information. He never painted over it, but instead, incorporated the work into the overall design scheme.

This was just the first of many places in which he would live as if in temporary guest quarters, flops, way stations, on his way to what permanent domicile he did not know, on his way to becoming he did not know what. At least now there was an inherent obsolescence; he would leave freshman housing in nine months. His refusal to personalize his surroundings and commit himself to them made some sense. Nine months. Why bother?

Willie Franklin was the first person through his door, and "I can't get the smell o' that woman offa me," the first words out of his mouth. The door had been slightly ajar. Willie pushed it open and stood on the threshold as it swung slowly and gently inward. Jessie stared at this wild-haired black man, a little shorter than he, but muscular and stocky, blue jeans and a T-shirt with an old jeans jacket thrown over it, big beige workboots, with a glint in his eye of the elfin, the devilish. He strolled in, looking all around as if on tour. He folded his arms across his chest and a la Jack Benny laid his thumb beneath his chin. He had a yellow electric guitar strapped around his neck.

"I like it," he said. "Fussy . . . but tasteful."

"I was working for that homey feel," Jessie said.

"And how you've achieved it," Willie replied. "If you're an artistically inclined lunatic. And you probably are."

They later became good friends; however, during those first few months of his freshman year, he had fallen in with an unamusing crowd. None were the decadent sons of the rich and famous, and none had suffered the emotional scarrings of boarding schools since birth. All dressed from mid-level department stores, with bents toward sporty casual wear. None ransacked church poor boxes for that tattered treasure that would give an ensemble that *je ne sais quoi*. They comported themselves with jocular good nature, that distant male camaraderie that always seemed forced and false to Jessie. So . . . in addition to his horrible roommates, he had bland friends, and began to fear that everyone at this exalted institution was as uninteresting as those with whom he spent his time: female history majors who played the cello; plain girls trying out for field hockey teams; male poli scis who took jobs in the cafeteria as part of their financial aid packages. They all thought him very nice and quiet, when in fact he was dumbstruck.

But then he met Willie, a Jimi Hendrix-obsessed electric guitar player who never had the faintest idea what courses he signed up for; who showed up for the first time at mid-terms, winging it, and generally passing. Further south, in Harvard Yard proper, he met new forms of life—forms new to him—the catalyst for which was Susannah.

He was headed to one of his off hour solitary meals in the freshman dining hall and while sliding his green fiberglass tray down the track of cylindrical aluminum poles, gazing through the snot shield at the various foods, opting for the passable lasagna, an enormous gash of red tore the room apart. It caught his eye (one would have had to have been blind for it not to) and he cast a glance. It was only a girl, a girl wearing an enormous, calf-length, fire engine red wool coat. He cast his eyes immediately back to the puddings and went about his business. Walking from the kitchen to the main hall he heard a bright, unapologetic, unembarrassed, "What's your name?"

He turned, almost dropping his tray, and faced the girl in the bright red coat. She had an equally bright, sincerely forced smile on her face, unlike any he had ever seen because he didn't resent its artificiality. Instead, he thought the fake smile a means to a benevolent, perhaps even noble end. Actually, she was flirting.

"Come, sit over here," she commanded as she strode toward a half-full table. No choice, he followed. Her name was Susannah.

After laying down her tray, she unwrapped her scarf and threw it in the corner of the table, removed her mittens and threw them on top of the scarf, and slid the coat off of her shoulders, simultaneously sinking into her chair. She introduced Jessie all around. One guy was French. Different, fine; and despite Jessie's still-unacknowledged and rarely considered sexuality, he had to recognize the Frenchman's beauty. One black-haired girl, Genevieve, with bright blue eyes and freckles, smiled vaguely and absently, as if she wasn't quite sure if the joke was on her, but the girl had enough training, enough of the artsy about her, had attended enough gallery openings and opera intermissions to smear looks of intelligence and comprehension across her underlying moronic vacancy. She was boinking the Frenchman. They'd hooked up the first week, and, Susannah later confided, had fucked incessantly since, about which Susannah was thoroughly pissed. She had seen him first. She introduced them. "Of course," she said, "he practically threw me to the ground and stepped on my windpipe to get to her." The last of the group had that same Genevieve-like look of refined moronism, except male, and therefore with foppish overtones—the unfiltered Gitanes between the first and index fingers, the half-mast lids and the thin lapeled suit jacket with the skinny tie, an emaciated frame that most thought wasting away from artistic sensitivity but actually the genetic curse of ectomorphism.

Susannah was beautiful and did most of the talking. Her skin was pale with an odd reddish smear on each cheek, and for the first time, as with the Annapolis moonlight, Jessie knew that blush was not a Max Factor invention. Her hair shone gold one minute, mahogany the next, like gold gilt paint on a canvas turned this way and that in the light. Its texture was silk, its colors and radiance and its idiosyncratic waves and dips and curls smally thrilling. She would shove a forkful of something in her mouth and then, sparked to comment, seemed to swallow it whole because her head would explode if she didn't speak immediately. She closed her eyes and her hands churned in front of her as if she did a '60s dance and the words just spewed out of her like coffee from a spittake. You couldn't help but be whisked up by her like big debris in a tornado and you couldn't help enjoying the ride despite the noise and inconvenience.

This was better. This was more like it. Visions of the bland crowd and their tryouts and their TVs and their Peter Frampton records immediately diminished as palpable horrors in the face of Susannah and these walking talking affectations. He'd come here, to Harvard, not to find things and people available at the local State U. He wanted, and had the right to expect the extraordinary. Poetry. Music. Madness. Anything beyond the mundane and mediocre. With Family he had *lived*, despite the fact he had taken it for granted at the time. Stifling evenings with his first crowd in which they popped popcorn to Led Zeppelin discs while getting stoned just bored him and angered him because he had known better. Didn't they realize he had spent afternoons on Assatigue Island fighting sandflies as big as his fist and chasing after wild ponies until he couldn't breathe? That he had sat on the rocks at Great Falls exhausted from the climb, his friends around him, the sky hovering lovingly above him, the silver water's fall filling his eyes and ears and the wind and the spray all touching him and not a thought, absolutely nothing his own in his head, just the sky and the wind and rocks and water? That he had found a rock island after rowing the canal and watched friends bathe, knowing no one would ever find it again?

These new people he might sink his teeth into. They wouldn't be like Family. That he could tell. Maybe Willie. There was something feral in these others, grasping. Each and every one of them needed something desperately that he or she should have possessed already, or never should have needed. There was no selflessness here, nothing unconditional, no "for better or for worse." These people chose you for what you had, for what strange or brilliant light you reflected on them. They were competitors, hangers-on and collectors—not friends—parasites without hope of satisfying hosts who joined in symbiosis.

Within a month or two, if he saw those folks with whom he spent those first months, they exchanged polite greetings and little else. They probably thought, "What happened to him? He used to be so nice."

The talk, with Susannah and her friends, was of Cocteau, a word Genevieve spat too often and with Inspector Clouseau-like vehemence enough to make you suspect she didn't know a thing about the man. Jessie was bursting to tell them (and they all played into his hands by demanding to know) that he was a writer—as were, of course, they all—symbolists, novelists, short storyists, diarists . . . He wondered if they were any good, and he wondered if they, like he, feared they were not; and he doubted the latter far more than the former.

Something brought the meal to an end. Certainly not a class. One never allowed those to interfere with meals. All rose and wrapped themselves in woolens. Jessie watched as Susannah pushed back her chair, her slim arms and shoulders rising, her lovely head atop them, rising . . . slowly rising . . . until finally, the biggest butt Jessie'd ever seen in his whole entire life appeared, like twin medicine balls you were scared shitless the coach would throw you in fourth-grade gym, like vibrating pumpkins in pants, the most bodacious, monumental *ass* anyone had ever seen. Virgin eyes bulged in shock.

Forks fell. Jessie was amazed. Later, he learned that his reaction was common, the shocked legion. Young men had known first love until they glimpsed Susannah's butt. Anatomical oddities usually don't warrant mention, but in this case the sheer ripeness of that thing defined her in an "if flesh could think" kind of way. She was deliciously, repulsively, sensual, at least to Jessie, to whom any scent of the carnal and fleshy was repulsive. Her body ruled her. She was completely of it, whereas most her age, most everyone of any age, seemed to wear theirs like an off-the-rack garment. And of that body—that rolling, waving, body—her ripe, dimpled butt and the snatch to which it unsubtly alluded, seemed her most significant parts. She made you feel like an animal, as if she were a chimp in estrus, and you should stick your snout right in that huge red thing she flashed around.

Once she attached herself, there was no escape, and Jessie sought none. Her persona was extraordinary, her mind utterly feminine, (female, of another species from his, this more noticeable with her than with any girl he knew), her chatter outrageously entertaining, her self-consciousness complete. That enormous fire-engine red coat in which she wrapped herself displayed the same iconographic power, the same new take on mythic themes that most of her clothes displayed. That coat reverberated with echoes of Riding Hood. It stunk with virginity and whoredom. Fluffy tops with useless lace things worn atop fatigues bespoke innocence and *coups d'état*. Jessie spoke little when he was with her. He generally nodded or smiled or shrugged his shoulders, mainly because he had no opinion on whether some Peter or Louis thought she was "a mindless bimbo" or not, and no, he couldn't muster any real enthusiasm over whether or not that skirt made her "look like a whale."

"You're just nodding your head and thinking 'I wish she'd shut up' I know but it's only because you're a boy—a man—because you're a man. I haven't gotten used to not calling them 'boys' yet. I still think of them as boys—*you* as boys. Oh God make me shut up. I don't know what I'm saying. My father is a 'man' Professor Siger is a 'man.' You have to be old and wizened to be a man, all the rest I call 'boy' so you won't be offended if I call you a boy . . ." she says, insisting he won't be offended by her *blatantly* offensive terms.

Jessie shrugged, in helplessness and exhaustion. She was an event.

One evening, she summoned Jessie down from South House to tend to her. She had a cold, feared "dying" or "floating away on rivers of snot," and desperately "craved" his company. He trudged the half mile from South House to the Yard, and found her in her bed, coverlets plentiful, pastels predominant, filthy stuffed animals strewn about, and impressionists on the walls. Her roommate, Beth, answered the door, a mildly humpbacked girl with a shock of kinky dirty-blonde hair done up in a bad afro. She looked like a witch. Jessie once saw her walking through Harvard

Square and thought, "Uh, that's strange, seeing a bag lady in the Square" until he got a little closer and recognized his classmate. She attempted the avant in her dress, but achieved the bedraggled. She became famous campus-wide for sporting the same oozing cold sore for six months running. They began to suspect she was leprous.

She answered the door with her short neck extended to its limit, her premature dowager's hump thrusting dagger-like at Jessie. "HI!" she brayed, expelling air enough to fill an inner tube, her tiny gray teeth exposed, her lips pulled back from them as if by fingers. "Soulee will be SOO happy to see you. Do you like that? Soulee? I made it up. I feel so guilty leaving her alone, but there's a reading and I'll just DIE if I miss it." And then in a bad Katherine Hepburn/Blanche Dubois, "I'll jus' DIE."

"Who's reading?" Jessie asked.

"Robert Lowell *and* Elizabeth Bishop. Do you believe it? Virginia Woolf CITY."

"That's not a reading," he said. "It's a drinking."

"Oh GOD, that's so FUNNY. You're so mean. Oh you've got to tell Soulee that one. She'll just DIE."

She dragged him into Susannah's bedroom.

"Susannah you've got to hear this it's soooo funny."

"Hi," Susannah said.

"Hi."

"I said I was going to a reading of Robert Lowell and Elizabeth Bishop and Jessie said . . . go on tell her what you said."

Susannah giggled to herself as Jessie lapsed into Shirley Temple, with a pixie's curtsy and a high voice, hands framing his face a la Jolson "And I said 'that's not a . . .'"

"Why that was very clever of you Shirley," Susannah said. "You deserve a treat!" She picked half a cookie off the bed and threw it at him. Clapping the back of his hands before his chest, he barked like a seal.

"I'm gonna tell *everyone* at the reading," Beth insisted. "You're so funny, Jessie," she giggled, exiting.

"Sometimes she is *so* awful," Susannah said once the front door slammed shut.

"Soulee? SOULEE?" he demanded. "Who, or perhaps what, is *Soulee?*"

"Oh God, she thinks it's cute. Little pet names."

A knock at the door.

"That's Sal," she said. "Will you let him in?"

Jessie was a bit perturbed that someone else had been invited. She knew him well enough by that time to realize he didn't get along with too many people. She considered herself privileged to be among them and harbored secret fears that he really loathed her. He had that effect on people; so few would have dared impose a stranger on him in this intimate a circumstance. He could tell by the look in her eye, though, that she had a plan. She acknowledged the risk, and chose to gamble.

Sal's hair, being shoulder-length, dark and wavy, cast a pre-Raphaelite shadow on his face, which was decidedly modern: ruddy, heavy eyebrows giving the cat-like eyes a malevolent glint, but the rest of the face soft and round. He had enormous feet, which jutted out at 45-degree angles, even when he walked. His legs being extremely long and thin, his feet looked uncommonly like a clown's. He wore regulation garb—dark crew neck over striped button-down, Levi's straight-leg cords.

He was shocked to see Jessie at the door. He looked suddenly up and down to verify he had the right room.

"Is that Sal?" Susannah howled from her bed.

"I guess you're Sal," Jessie said, gesturing toward the bedroom. "I'm Jessie."

"Is she dead yet?"

"Not sure."

They marched into Susannah's room, where, from her bed, she smiled. She beamed in fact. The fact that fur had not yet flown meant her little plan might work.

She met Sal with the same bulldozing style she used on Jessie. He was another she thought looked "interesting." Which was another way of saying she wanted to sleep with him. She had an amazing ability to lust after those of questionable sexuality. Some of Sal's habits and movements, the way he minutely shook his head while simultaneously swiping hair from his cheek with the back of his hand, the occasional limp wrist, the way his head sometimes wobbled jerkily on his neck, some of these were suspiciously feminine. He used to keep snakes in high school, and walked with his nose in the air, which made his figure particularly odd—thin, long spindly legs with the toes pointing outward and the knees bending deeply with each step—a near-parody of a walk, but with an equally exaggerated hauteur in the carriage of his head. One would have thought he was joking.

They both gleaned her plan. Jessie could just hear her. "Oh they're so much alike, they're, like, *cloned*. They're both complete cynics and hate everything." She insisted they'd get along famously. Being complete cynics and hating everything, their initial impulses were to loathe one another, just to refute Susannah's implied self-congratulatory insight into their psyches. Ordinarily, Jessie, at least, would have succeeded, and they would have become bitter enemies; but it didn't happen that way. She sent them out for ice cream, suggesting, "take your time."

If forced, they would have admitted they intrigued each other. They'd been with each other for fifteen minutes, and neither had heard the other say anything stupid. Both held the human race in contempt for various injuries done to them (none one of which they consciously acknowledged) and thought that most human words had been stewed too long in vats of foolishness, like good meat in rank juices. Their judgments were swift, and generally irrevocable. Once they condemned, redemption was infeasible. They were, actually, very much alike.

"Do you think she could be any more obvious?"

"I think she wants us to get to know each other," Jessie said.

"She is so irritating sometimes. There's something really . . . *gross* about her, don't you think? So . . . *girl*.

You know what I mean?"

Jessie: "Like everything she wears, pink and frilly?"

"Yeah," Sal replied, "and those pictures on the wall, and the books she reads, everything . . ."

Pause.

"Where're you from?" Sal asked.

"The Colonel lives in DC now. That's where I went to high school, but I lived a lot of different places."

"The Colonel?"

"My father." Jessie never mentioned his mother save to say, "She died when I was younger."

"You call him the Colonel?"

"I don't like him."

"My Dad's a real SOB sometimes, but he's really cool, too. He doesn't care about *anything*." Sal shook his head with an odd vehemence, the face momentarily a mask of angry disbelief, immediately replaced with one of amused admiration. "I don't think he's ever called me by my name. It's 'hey' or 'hey idiot' or 'where's the little shit?'"

"Didn't that piss you off?"

"No. I thought it was kinda cool."

"Is your mother still alive?" Jessie asked.

"Yeah. She's a nutbar though."

Jessie chuckled.

"No, really," Sal corrected. "She cracked up when I was little. She thought I was the anti-Christ or something and tried to kill me."

"You're kidding."

"No, I'm not. They locked her up. It was back in

the snake pit days and they fried her brains. She's kind o' vague these days."

He paused.

"It's uncanny, though," he added, "I look just like her."

Sal grew up in the "poor" section of a very rich town. His father, Giovanni, was a handsome first-generation American of Sicilian parents who'd fought in World War II in the South Pacific, in the jungles, and once told his sons' friends about days and days and weeks of trudging through humid green jungles and having the clothes on your back mildew, your skin itself mildew, all stinking so bad you almost made yourself sick. He didn't think he had killed anyone. He stayed in the background. He shot his gun, but blindly.

He may not have personally shot anyone, but he saw things. He saw heaps and piles of dead men. Bodies exploded in the heat. The blood and flesh turned blue and black. Every kind of jungle creature invaded them and fed on them. He saw young American boys climb atop these foul heaps as if playing "king o' the hill" and claw the solid gold fillings from heads, the flesh on which split and cracked like rotting vegetation at the touch. And after seeing that he knew he had been right all along.

Giovanni had been a bastard waiting to happen. He assigned no purpose to this confusion of a life, had found no dignities to be wrung from it. He disgusted himself for the same reasons others disgusted him—

because he was small. But his parents and his church and those all around him had hopes and dreams to which they clung tenaciously and a faith they followed with the fervor of madmen. They took jobs and had children and acted as if their tiny little spots in this big world meant something profound. He didn't know how they did it. He couldn't find their zeal within himself. He couldn't convince himself to strive and seek and succumb to organizing principles so flimsy and threadbare they hardly began to cover the random, mismatched agglomeration of things and happenings that comprised this world. Without all the parental/religious strictures and bonds they might be free to seek what pleasures there were, which was all there was to do. But they refused to be free. For that he could not forgive them, and he wanted to hold them in contempt, but he was scared. He could not prove them wrong. He'd read their laws and bibles and knew they'd have words of refutation handy and he had neither the counters to convince them nor the evidence to prove them wrong. Until he had, he would live fearfully and silently, because deep down he was scared to death they might be right. So he pretended to abide and believe. He enlisted in the Army when the country went to war, and with that act forged the club with which to flog himself again and again because he knew he sought proof of valor's existence. He wanted the cheapest wartime sentiments. He wanted the hero to die to save his comrade. He wanted to see that. He grabbed at this chance of a lifetime to join the herd at the troughs and saltlicks because, to him, it *was* the brass ring and maybe if he saw that act of honor he wouldn't have to cart around this hairball of bitter, bitter emptiness. He could spit it out before he choked on it.

And when he smelled the stench and vomited, and again at the sight of corpses festering, and when he saw living men dancing on them as if they were home, well, then he knew. A smile, a smirk, fixed itself on his face, and it never left. He carried it for the rest of his life. He guarded his life well, took no chances with it. He would stay alive, a smirk on his face, and watch, as one would beasts in cages, and gloat and know that he was right and watch the fools and say, "I told you so. I knew all along."

With his veteran's benefits, he became a dentist, the better to remind him, every day, of what he, and so few others, knew. He took a wife, an Italian beauty, for whom he cared little, the better to savor the jest. Soon, he looked just like one of them, except for that odd smile forever on his face.

*

Sal laughed, as if impressed with an absurdity. "After he divorced my mother, he married the dental hygienist he had been fucking for years, and the incredible part was, she went to high school with my sister. She used to come over to the house to play with his own daughter." Sal squealed with laughter.

Jessie smiled, and shook his head and shrugged resignedly.

Sal loathed his mother. He described her as some harridan, but Susannah, having met the woman, insisted she was a perfectly pleasant, well-kept, middle-class older woman. "Although," she added, "of course she can't compete with the father, whom he thinks is some unearthly stud with a penis that would shame a moose."

Sal and Jessie talked philosophy. Sal planned to major in it, mainly because he knew he was smart and thought it might hold answers. It seemed offbeat to him.

"I know nothing about it," Jessie said. "I have very little patience with it."

"I love it," Sal enthused. "How could you have no patience with something that tells you how to live"

"I don't need or want anyone telling me how to live. When someone does a good enough job of it so they never die, him I'll listen to, but until then, it's just jacking off as far as I'm concerned."

"You don't think anyone can tell you anything about living?"

"Not that I would listen to."

"Jesus," Sal said.

"What?"

"You might be even more arrogant than I am."

Chapter XI

GHOSTS

Willie came and went. He knew about Susannah and Sal and the others, but rarely socialized with the group. He rarely kept to campus, traipsing instead to girls' schools for sex or haunting the nearby Jazzbo School of Music, searching bulletin boards for "guitarist wanted" signs.

Willie examined Jessie's record collection and found it lacking, so he force-fed him Hendrix and told him tales of Miles. They cut an odd figure, the stocky Willie in quasi-military and the feline Jessie in effete bohemian attire. Susannah and the others feared Willie, not for anything he had done or said—but because he was black. They feared Jessie too, but he gave them reason. If someone approached in the dining hall and asked, "mind if I joined you?" he often said, "I'd rather you wouldn't." For most, that sufficed. They gladly sat elsewhere. Some, however, pressed the point, like Sam, the son of a Broadway maven. "Why?" Sam foolishly asked.

"Because, Sam," Jessie replied, "I don't like you."

"You know, that's a really shitty thing to say . . ."

"Why, Sam?"

Sam paused, pondering. "'Cause it is!"

"It's not shitty, Sam. It is truthful. I don't like you. Most things about you annoy me. I was perfectly happy to keep that to myself until you stupidly instigated this conversation, the doing of which is a perfect example of why you annoy me."

Everyone agreed with Jessie. Sam *was* incredibly annoying; but others would not have said so, not to his face; some because it would break tender rules of decorum and others because his father was powerful, and they feared Sam might be useful. The rules did not interest Jessie. For him, niceties and conventions, after a point (the point of politeness), had no place. He believed firmly in politeness. He resented those who couldn't take a hint and let him practice it. Sam had been rude. He had asked a question, had received an answer, and should have left it at that. Instead, he protested because the answer was not to his liking. Well, that was just tough. Ask a "yes" or "no" question, and the "no" is a possibility you should be prepared to graciously accept. A quirky personal system, but one Jessie employed because he so loved opportunities to tell people to blow it out their asses. It was his revenge against the world. He just wondered how he got away with it.

He finally figured it out when, arriving late for a marathon lunch, guilt-ridden titters greeted him. Susannah, Sal, and others sat there, hands over mouths and guilty grins as if his arrival were particularly ironic—i.e., he had been spoken about.

"What's so funny," Jessie asked obligatorily as he set his tray down and took a seat.

They all looked at one another, and a new wave of giggles overtook them.

"My fly's not open 'cause I'm not wearing any underwear and my dick would be cold. I don't have a cold so there's no visible snot, so one of you must have placed a 'Kick me' sign on my back. Please remove it."

Nothing. The giggly mirth turned darker. Notes of fear and dread hummed softly.

"Beth?" Jessie said, attacking the weakest link. She was about to speak when Susannah interjected, thinking it better to sweeten the truth than have Beth take a fall over it.

"We were talking about black people."

Pause.

"Oh them," Jessie said. "Yes, my dick *is* enormous, and yes, I will tan. Does that cover it?"

"Nothing like that," Susannah whined, insulted. "We were talking about someone else and your name came up, and it seemed odd."

"Oh. Now I understand."

"We thought it was odd that your name should come up," she clarified; and Beth blurted: ". . . like you were really a black person or something."

CONTEMPLATIVE SILENCE, PLEASE.

It all made sense, suddenly, like a gigantic 2,000-piece puzzle of "Desmoiselle D'Avignon" finally revealing its form, like a geometric proof's conclusion appearing suddenly as if predestined.

With apartheid-like largesse, they had conferred on him the role of Honorary White. They, and how many others, he wondered? They avoided Willie because he remained the "other," because on him they, for whatever reason, did not pin that honorary distinction, the granting of which was nothing conscious or considered. It just was. They had no insights into, nor interest in, its origins. The act was involuntary, and thus effortless, like breathing. Certain fundamentals had been folded into their beings and could not be taken out, eggwhite to batter in the creation of a white-person soufflé: they assume themselves inherently different from, and generally superior to, all Afro-Americans (aka, "The Fundamental Principal of Whiteness").

The black men and women whom the students at that table were forced by personal experience to consider equals got immediately reclassified as Honorary White (thus not disturbing the Fundamental Principal). These reclassified Africans gained acknowledgment as biologically and philosophically similar to White Americans (i.e., Humans), and thus hot house exotics to be indulged, pampered and admired like full-bred cockapoos.

Jessie realized that the Fundamental Principal was just one piece of a large puzzle, since, symbiotically, he had been raised to consider *himself* inferior to white people—less than—in some fundamental way. After all, since earliest childhood he was bombarded with images of normality, regularity, power, glory, genius, and beauty, precious few of which contained anyone who looked like him. The images Afro-Americas saw of themselves often depicted criminals, victims, poverty, ignorance, and blight.

The line in the '60s read: "Yes, you too little boy, can grow up to be President of the United States." This was America's glory. This was central to all American propaganda, the most ardent disseminator of which was the American public school system. Yet, Jessie and every other American child descended from African slaves knew at the time that the supposedly all-inclusive generic "you" did not include them. He did not even qualify for inclusion under the linguistic umbrella of generic pronouns. (Of course, all women were excluded.) He did not count. Yet, his exclusion did not taint America's glory in the popular mind— which meant that he and his ilk must have been especially insignificant.

He never recognized social divisions between himself and the majority. He attended their schools. He competed successfully with them. His skin was darker, and prettier. That was all. Both Grandier and Lulene insisted on his potential superiority to anyone in any endeavor. This insistence bordered on the psychopathic at times, in extreme circumstances, desperate measures. Yet, even that insistence whispered the fact of white dominance and control.

Both beyond and within the racial frame, however, he truly thought himself better. Missy and Honey and Lulene and Aunt Ethel were black, but they were *them* and being American descendants of African slaves was a big part of that magic. There was no untangling the two. He had lived a resoundingly middle-class life. Want never touched him, and plenty often did. He felt no less comfortable in a room full of blacks than in a room full of whites. He resented the term "brother," thinking it close to blackmail. Its own little HUAC, a loyalty test and oath all rolled into one. He would brook no such assumed familial insistence from his own blood relations, much less strangers with like ancestry. While whites threw comments like "not really black," and some black folks said the same for the reasons above.

"Since when are you the arbiters of what is and is not black?" he asked. Their secretive smiles contorting into embarrassed facial twitches.

"You say that only because you can't think you're better." He paused. He smiled as he looked at their faces. It was a shark's smile at the sight of a body bag of blood thrashing madly in the water.

"And," he added, standing for effect, an exit line, "you're not."

"White people," Willie later said, "*slay* me."

Willie had been raised in Newark with a Rhodes Scholar brother and some phenomenal IQ thing going. His brother did everything right. He got the A's, excelled at sports, majored in Poli Sci, and ran for offices he won.

Willie was obsessed with music. He didn't feel right with Jessie's literary friends. He thought them foolish. "They're playing," he said. "They're just playing. When push comes to shove, they'll go to law school." The bourgeois black crowd bored him senseless. Sal said Jessie might be the ultimate aesthete. If so, Willie took a close second. He'd sought transcendence just about everywhere—drugs, philosophy, literature, physics, you name it. Just as Jessie sought heaven by climbing a mountain of paper and film reels, Willie would ride the guitar strings.

Willie first took him to the music library, an act that changed Jessie's life. There, in one place, were countless records, classical and jazz, spanning the history of recorded music. You took records into rooms and listened. Willie led, and Jessie followed. You might try some middle Miles," Willie'd say, and Jessie was off.

Willie would disappear for days at a time. God knows where. Sometimes, he found gigs around Boston. Other times, he showed up looking like hell. Asked where he had been, he just sat, looking ragged, a Cheshire Cat smile on his face. Together they decided Bryan Ferry was God, for lines like, "This is tomorrow calling/Wishing you were here," and turning "Let's Stick Together" into a callow playboy's whine. He didn't have Jessie's good-boy grounding. There was nothing bourgeois in his thirst for anarchy. He *would* create it, if given a chance. He had the stomach for it. Jessie envied him that. Jessie dreamt vague and future rebellions, subtle ones, seductive ones made sweet to standard tastes by his personal sugar-coatings. He dreamt a coward's rebellions, while Willie dared a rebel's. Jessie couldn't even dream them. They weren't in him. He'd been raised never to withstand the disdain.

One night, Willie came to Jessie's room when Sal and he were warm from red wine and they talked about scary things they'd seen. Willie told them a story.

"Now, you ever been to Newark?"

"Uh-uh."

"Keep it that way. You?" he said to Sal.

"Yeah. Some of it looks like Dresden . . . bombed-out buildings."

"One night, three o'clock in the morning, my car stops. Just stops, right there in downtown Newark. Everything's either boarded up or gated up and shut down. There's no one out there. But that's okay. I'm used to this. I grew up here. I'm a big guy. Chances are, no one's gonna fuck with me. I'm just gonna go find a phone that works, get someone to pick me up. I'd have to wait 'till daylight to get someone to tow the car. No tow's crazy enough to come out there at night.

"So I'm walkin' down the street . . . I pass a phone but it's all ripped out. I'm scared I'll wind up walkin' all the way home. It's real quiet. Of course, I hear little things, little bumps and knocks around corners. My own footsteps sounded unbelievably loud, like they were someone else's, probably 'cause I was listening so hard. So I'm just walking, trying to keep calm.

"I turn a corner and across the street, I see this guy come out of a doorway. It was cold and he was wearing a black hat and a long coat. I couldn't see much of him, but from the back of his neck I could tell he was white. Now this had to be one crazy stupid fucker. What the hell was some white guy doin' in downtown Newark at three o'clock in the morning?"

Willie shrugged. "He came out of a building so I thought about asking if I could use his phone, but shit, this guys white and coming out of a doorway here? He has to be dangerous or nuts, so I figured I'd best keep walking. Out of the corner of my eye, I got the idea that he'd turned in the other direction, walking away from me and around a corner."

"After a minute, I start regretting not talking to that guy. Maybe he just didn't know where he was, and second, it was fuckin' cold. So I start walking a little faster.

"Up ahead, I see this guy come out of a building, wearing a black hat and a long coat, and I can only see his back," he paused. "But from the back of the neck I could tell he was white.

"So I've seen two white guys in downtown Newark in the middle of the night." He shook his head. "Uh-uh." So I stop and stare at this one. He turns away from me and walks down the street. I yelled after him."

"Hey, stupidwhiteboy?" Jessie asked.

"He ignored me. Kept walkin, and he was walking fast; turned a corner. So I ran after him. I ran up to the corner and turned . . . and there he was, standing, about ten yards ahead of me, with his back to me. Stock still. I stopped short, in mid-step. I looked like one o' those catalogue ads."

"Sears," Sal laughed, miming the man-in-motion male model pose.

"Right," Willie said, a little dismissive, Sal trying too hard to amuse.

"I just stand there a minute, staring, but this guy doesn't move. 'I saw you come out of a building back there.' I started talking . . . 'My car broke down. Do you have a phone I could use to call someone to come pick me up?'

"He didn't move. I mean not a muscle. He stood there like he was waiting for something, his back to me, not even acknowledging me. With that black hat and coat on, he looked like somethin' out of an old black-and-white movie. I took a step toward him, and like someone switched him on, he walks, that same fast walk, no build-up, like he never stopped.

"So, fuck it, I turned around and kept on going. Whatever this guy's problem was, it wasn't mine. I just had to get home.

"I turn the corner and BAM! He's standing right in front of me, a foot away. He had his back to me again so I could see that white bit of neck. But then he turned around and I froze.

"It was empty where a face should have been. Not even flesh, but light, with shape. It's stupid, but I put up my hands, as if to fight. Just a reflex."

He paused and rubbed his forehead.

"I smashed into a brick wall ten feet away like someone had swung it at me. I stung all over for a moment, and then I was out.

"When I woke up it was daylight. I was lying up against a wall. I had blood on me. I stank. I'd pissed in my pants."

"You were tripping," Jessie said.

"I swear. Nothing. I had nothing. No booze, drugs, nothing. Nothing."

He paused. Jessie and Sal didn't know how much to believe. Jessie'd never seen him this sincere, not gravely, matter of factly so.

"I saw that guy again. A couple years later. That I know. And I think I saw him one more time, but I can't be sure. He's around, though. I know that. I might turn a corner and open a door and bam, there he'll be. Maybe next time he'll finally do whatever he's been waiting around and watching for."

"Which is?" Sal asked.

Willie just shrugged. It was the only time Jessie saw him look scared.

One day, Willie left campus and never came back. A week, a month, no visits, no drop-ins. He disappeared. Jessie asked around, but no one had seen him. No one knew where he had gone.

Willie was different, a little special. As much as Jessie loved the Family, Willie was special because he knew what a saxophone meant, and what Mahalia Jackson sounded like. He, too, believed in ghosts.

*****

Jessie got used to meeting lute playing proto-fascist drag queens with phenomenal IQ's because, well, that's just the kinda place Harvard was, priding itself on its "interesting" student body. Thus, Bobby shocked no one, as he, curly blond hair and zit-strewn face atop a skinny 6'2" frame, strolled into the dining hall in a gorgeous off-the shoulder black taffeta with matching heels and black hose. This was lunch. Dinner would surely be something special.

They all got used to the diminutive fellow who specialized in ill-conceived theater pieces, who watched his own productions while madly waving his arms and bouncing up and down with delight like a demented puppet soon to embark on a hatchet murder spree.

Since Jessie spent a lot of time at Adams House dorm, noted for its artistic occupants, he shared space with the school's openly gay men. It was the "first contact," and as acceptance of his leanings became more difficult to suppress, he feared being like them should he succumb. Little did he allow for the general personality exaggerations of which he, and everyone he knew was guilty. In short, he was looking for means to forestall the inevitable, and he almost found them. Scarves flew in all directions when they walked in a room. Hips followed. Not a hair out of place, they managed to get through days without putting a crease in a button-down shirt. Their faces were blue. Jessie and Sal wondered if there was a special homosexual shaving implement that resulted in a perfect smoothness and a Fred Flintstone bluish tinge where stubble should have been. As a matter a fact, a few came out of the closet and soon thereafter developed blue faces. Jessie wouldn't admit he was flattered when one called him the man he most wanted to seduce.

They all tried too hard. Desperation lived there. They all had dreams to fulfill, and this august institution was their first step toward them. God forbid they should stumble and fall. "Such great promise," they'd say, "Who would have thought it would come to so little? Failure hounded them all like death does the ancient and infirm. Jessie had already tasted some. He'd arrived there The Writer but had had to admit that his words were not good enough. A wall always plopped itself between him and what he had to say. And he knew it was him that put it there. Without that wall, he would have stood exposed and naked. And he could not withstand that. Damaged and sad. There was no dignity in it. With pictures, he thought could stand at safe distance, like a God.

Chapter XII

ACID MUTANTS

Standing behind the desk at Harvard's Hilles Library, a hushed, beige, ambiently humming structure, Phyllis let her black cashmere boat neck slip off one raised shoulder and let the other shoulder dip seductively, her neck-length, Henna-highlighted hair dripping Veronica Lake-like over one eye. With her tall thin frame the pose worked from the neck down. Were it not for that nose, she might have pulled it off. With it, however, she looked more the fetching piglet than the vamp.

"I want to go through life like this," she told Jessie of the pose. They'd finagled shared job-shifts. Word had spread and students strenuously avoided the reserved-books desk because of the monsters who worked it.

"Your nose won't let you," he said.

"We should have kids," she told him. "Between your nose going south and mine north, we might produce a straight one."

She had spent her life in spitting distance of money, right on the edge of it, but never feeling its electric, fibrous touch on her own naked flesh. She had never, as she put it, "wiped herself" with it. She knew Long

Island like the back of her hand. Give her a street address and she quoted gross income and told you what art they had on their walls. Her mother sent her to Harvard to snag a rich man, and thus redeem the family from the horrid middle-income bracket to which the dead father had condemned it. Phyllis was bright, but nonetheless her mother's lessons had pitched petty factions into battle over her self-image. With powder-puff artillery and lipstick-swords, one side fought for veined hands with perfect nails dripping in sapphires ringed with tiny diamonds and a blood alcohol level that would kill a seaman, and the other side for tight skirts, chewing gum, spike heels and a prominent place in a secretarial pool.

"My ambitions," she admitted, "aren't even worthy of the term."

A couple of students they ignored stood patiently at the desk hoping to check out some books. They knew that pushing the point would gain them nothing.

"Have you noticed," Jessie began, thinking about helping the students, "the number of maimed who've come in here today?"

Phyllis' eyes grew wide. Her head bobbed stiffly causing her hair to agitate as if it didn't know in which direction to twirl. "It's amazing!" she cried. "I'm expecting a headless guy any minute. Broken arms, crutches, a neck brace . . ."

"They must be Kennedys" Jessie suggested.

Phyllis' mouth dropped open. Just then, Jessie noticed a pair of crutches clicking toward the door, a one-legged person leaning on them.

"That was Teddy Kennedy, Jr.!" she hissed.

"Oh my God . . ."

*****

Gary was a long-haired, owl-eyed fellow whose mind worked wonders in its peregrinations, like a prism, taking a notion and reflecting it into a big, bright rainbow. Jessie loved this. There was such a little boy in him when he opened his big eyes even more brightly and leaned toward you with that lurid smile, like a jovial madman, and let loose with one of his patented "what ifs." Somewhere in him, Jessie knew an attraction existed. There was the wounded puppy in him. Gary needed so nakedly, and Jessie could not resist open, naked, need, longing, hurt, outstretched arms and pleading eyes, all the things he couldn't have, all the things for which he had made himself too proud.

Jessie and Sal stopped to fetch Gary on the way to a pizza joint. Jessie didn't believe it that Gary had taken to burning his flesh with cigarettes. Both he and Sal felt tense, the alleged burnings foremost in their minds, but playing nonchalant as they walked along gossiping, talking shop, and pretending strained silences meant nothing.

Fairly late at night, the large empty pizza shop glowed with a Hopper-esque glare. They sat in a booth.

Gary put his hands on the table and Jessie saw the round patches of raw flesh, three on one hand, two on the other.

Jessie pictured it—Gary sitting, shirtless on his bed, holding the cigarette like an amateur, between the thumb and first fingers, taking a few drags and coughing a bit, like he always did when he tried to smoke, but then putting it right back in his mouth again to puff some more. When the end was red and hot, he would stare at it, wide eyed, imagining the burn, knowing it would touch and change his tender skin, fascinated by that. He would bend far over, his head as close to his hand as he could get it, and bring the cigarette close to the flesh, the skin abstracted and strange in close-up. Then the two would come together, the flesh and the fire. He would neither cringe nor wince. His hand would not move. He would watch, an inch away, as the fire changed the skin, a sizzling sound, soon muffled as the ember seared deeper. Smoke rising, full of that acrid burning flesh smell, like hair on fire. He would then pull the cigarette away, and study the circle of screaming flesh, ash and black at its edges, pain thrashing within its circumference like electricity.

Jessie stared at the scars and grew angry. Those images flashed in his mind and incensed him. The dispassion, the clinical air, the weakness and pain so gluttonously indulged frightened and disgusted him. The threat hit too close to home.

"I don't believe you did that," he said.

Gary grinned, more like a leer. "I think they look

kinda neat," he said of the scars, "like flying saucer landing pads or something."

"Why did you do that?"

Getting uncomfortable, Gary shrugged.

"It really is a little strange, Gary," Sal said.

"I was curious."

"Curious? People skydive out of curiosity. They don't burn holes in themselves. You wanted attention that bad? Call someone, go see a shrink for Christ's sake, they're paid to pay attention to you."

Jessie's fury surprised even him, as if the unacknowledged pain on display were a direct threat.

"I didn't want attention."

"Why the hand then, why not your thigh or someplace where people wouldn't notice?"

Gary looked at Sal, who had nothing to offer him. He cast his eyes on the table and shrugged again.

They heard no more of Gary wounding himself. He bore no more visible scars.

*****

In the dead-of-winter sophomore year, Family John came down from Bennington College with Family Emily who'd been visiting him. They came to Cambridge to accompany Jessie on a hallowed rite of studentdom— his first acid trip. John and Emily had been together all these years, since high school, on and off. John was still the same, and Emily was still the same, except she had cramps and looked a bit bluish.

"'The stars who play with laughing Sam's dice . . .'" Willie quoted Hendrix when he handed Jessie two hits of acid. "Acid's the *only* drug because it doesn't really do anything except make what's already there stand up and scream at you. It *is* a mind-expanding drug," he had said. That thought terrified Jessie.

"I don't want my mind expanded. What's to keep it from bursting?"

"It's a chance you gotta take," Willie said. "It's a roll of the dice. You can have great trips, like rolling through daisies and peace and love and all that crap. Or, you could be covered with spiders strapped to an electric chair. I've had both."

He left Jessie, suggesting he take half a hit, being a first-timer. Foolishly, Jessie took it mid-shift at Hilles library.

"Are you okay?" Phyllis asked as he rushed at hyperspeed through the reserved stacks. He giggled at her. After a while, the buzzing in his head grew very, very loud, and his head felt like it was shrinking while being simultaneously lifted off his shoulders and carried about one foot above his neck.

"Do you have a fever?" Phyllis asked.

He giggled at her, and his eyes might have rolled back into his head.

"Are you possessed? Should I fetch a priest?"

He motioned her to the back of the stacks, several students standing at the desk, waiting, while the staff disappeared.

"I took this acid," he said. "I think it kicked in."

"Oh," she shouted, "Oh!" her head bobbing and her hair bouncing madly. "Drugs! Acid! How positively bohemian! Jessie, I'm so impressed."

"Yeah, well, I think I better go now."

"Oh, yes. Before the books sprout wings and you do moose impersonations or something. Go. Enjoy."

"Thanks."

He got to his room to find Emily writhing on the bed clutching her stomach, explaining how she had puked on the subway. John sat on the floor with a book in his hand.

"You got that acid?" he asked.

Jessie gave him the remaining acid for him and Emily to split. He then resumed walking up and down the hall, his hands extending, a la Marcel Marceau, to occasionally push against some unseen obstacle. He simply could not stand still. There was motion inside his head and his limbs followed involuntarily like a dog's tail does its body.

"I have got to get out of here," Jessie said between his teeth. "Are you ready yet?"

"Just wait a minute," Emily said, I should be okay in a little while. I wanna trip, too"

"Now!" he said. "I have to go NOW."

"Will you be okay?" John asked Emily.

"I'll be fine. Go ahead. But leave me the hit."

"You took some, too," Jessie said to John. "How can you just *sit* there?"

"Come on," John said.

Winters in Cambridge were lovely sometimes, with the fresh snow coating everything and its white refracting street light which hung in the air like theatrical scrim.

Jessie felt better outside, the heavy wools around him and the effort of lifting each booted foot high off the ground with every step, out of the snow, and planting it back in it—that satisfied his motion cravings. Calmer, he looked around him, at a cross-country skier sliding across the snow with his two long canes; a car almost obscured by the powdery bright all over it. These things seemed distant—not themselves somehow. They seemed more than themselves. They seemed a part of everything; and they echoed, and ached and moaned for everything of which they were a part, like those horrified voices in Penderewski might.

He could not look at them. He couldn't look at anything because doing so opened up some private hell and all its screams, it's spittle on his face, its roar ready to burst his ears until they bled. Nothing was just itself. With his head buzzing and vibrating, he stared at the snow, feeling trapped within himself, within his bones and bowels and skin, looking through eyes as if they were holes torn in a curtain from under which he couldn't escape. No matter how hard he fumbled and threw reams and reams of cloth, its hem could not be found. He stopped trying, and looked out and saw nothing he knew, nothing warm or familiar, just objects that stung his mind.

Each thing was too much a part of every other thing. That man over there and the coat he wore were each part of the woman down the street, who may have sewn that coat together, and how much did she make, that woman? Enough to live? And how many mouths did she try to feed on what little she made? The guy might have worked for the company that owned the company that built the car she drove, which somebody else welded who might live down the way. What was his tale? What hurts had he buried along the way? Who loved him? Did anybody love him?

Images flashed at him like those in hysterically edited films—sparks from welding tools, a baby crying, a big tree felled and a saw taken to it—lightning bolts of images, too much, with each tied to the other by some long string that he could see now, which led his eyes from thing to thing like the road hurls a race car from cone to cone, only Jessie had no control. His headfirst plunge was free-fall and he wanted to scream but he knew it wouldn't help, so he kept his mouth shut and his eyes on the snow, the clean white snow which was the only thing not screaming, everything else mewling and howling at the top of its lungs like moaning banshees or hellhounds.

He walked next to John in silence. John said he was hungry and walked Jessie into a Chinese restaurant. Jessie looked up and his head almost split open. He put his hands to his ears because every nook and cranny was filled with things and people screaming their tales and horrors at him as if they'd waited a thousand lifetimes for someone who could hear them. He closed his eyes and turned around, his head shaking "no no no no no no no" as he shambled out the door and John followed.

He didn't think he could stand it. He felt as if he had been this way forever, and would be this way as long and he was ready to do anything to change that. John talked him out of checking himself into the school clinic, but he wanted so badly for those lightning flashes and voices to stop. He didn't know how much longer he could listen. He was scared they wouldn't go away, that they might stick, jam, torment him forever, until he might die for want of peace. It was like Willie's fear of seeing the face of the man in black. Jessie dreaded hearing what the screams were trying to say.

Finally, when he knew the sounds would torment him forever, they shifted. They quieted. The shriekings became urgent whispers, and those he could bear. He could look around him now, and did not want to hide or rip his own eyes and ears from his head. He and John stopped in a small Cambridge mall, a cheesecake place downstairs, a few shops selling Merrimeko and crafts, full of rails painted fire engine red, exposed brick and iron balustrades. They sat at the top of the stairs, and watched the people walk beneath them. A woman walked by with enormous antennae and wings that matched her purse. The man next to her had the shell of a beetle. The whole procession, every one of them, had enormous ears or dinosaur's feet, or chicken's lips or a fishface. Like peacocks they walked by, completely unaware, or maybe even proud of, their outlandish mutations; and Jessie sat on the steps above, watching them walk by, delighted by their oddity, amused by their insouciance, their arrogance in the face of their own utter foolishness. How could they walk about so sillily and think themselves so grand? He sat up there for hours, feeling kindly and amused.

Willie barged into Jessie's room next morning with thorazine tablets, just in case Jessie lay on the floor, freaking out completely, his failure to make lunch having put Willie on alert.

His head clear, only fatigue left over from the night before, Jessie knew he would never take that drug again. Once was enough. There were things he did not wish to know, things he did not want to see; mostly things inside himself. You see, he knew it wasn't that different. What he saw the previous night, those feelings he had of things and people not quite what they seem but simply façades and representations of so much more—things that would, if you listen, speak to you; that would, if they felt they could, howl at you for no other reason than the fact that you could hear them, feel their pain, know it like few would. They were the personification of hurt. It wasn't that different from his normal state, you see, except most of the time, he could screen them out. Only momentarily would he hear their roar, as if a door had opened and immediately slammed shut again; he could bludgeon them to silence, as he had Gary. Sometimes, he heard the murmurs, all just beneath the surface, like putting his ear to the wall, but he built something tall and strong between him and that which would have him for its (or their) own, monopolize his mind with its anguished ravings.

This, right here, was the march of the acid mutants.

PART III

Chapter XIII

TO WEAR THE DOGMASK
(or)
CLOWNSQUAD

"I never knew Ther names. The nurses laug-
fed at me.

"The jujes didnt know. They had no
right to sit and juje me. I took the bulets. I
shot the gooks like they told me too. I did
what they sayd.

"The nurses give me shots to keep me
qwiet. They don't want you to no. they dont
want you to no. it doesnt matter cus i dont
wanna tell. not yet. Youl know when I'm
ready."

At Jessie's mailroom job at the TV network, all
sorts of odd things came through. They got fan letters
from people who obviously thought TV characters
were real; asking where the funerals would be held
for characters who had died. They got viciously racist
letters complaining of too many "niggers" on this show
or that.

And then came these post cards and photocopied
sheets bearing Pittsburgh postmarks, from a man who
didn't sign his name.

Reading between the lines, it seemed he might be in a VA hospital. He was a Vietnam veteran, and while obviously insane, wrote with a twisted grace.

> "They came for me when i was little. They shoved me in school and beat me. after a while it didnt mater any more. i jus looked at em. i wanted to shove my dick down their throats until they made that gagging noise i liked to hear.
>
> "they came for me in the jungle and i almost got out alive.
>
> "they dont no im here yet. i dont no what it means. i jus no that all my life i been fighting somethin."

And then:

> Me: I told you they'd come after me.
>
> bilding: Its becuase of the war.
>
> Me: i didnt kill anyone.
>
> bilding: Liar.
>
> Me: it doesnt matter. ive got a gun now. ican defend myself.
>
> building: its no diffremt. That wont help.
>
> ME: I'm the enemy, they wear tight uniforms. i can see ther tits through the univorm and they dont even care. ther

whores. i'd like to suck on em. those big tits.

building: they wont let you fuck em. they
hate you.

ME: I don kno why they hate me. I don know
who did this to me. I musta let em. I couldn't
stop em. I tried.

…And finally…

"this is the last letter. Theres no reason to
rite any more.

I tole em everything i had to say. they no
now. Its there own business what they do.
the Tv will tell them..

"i didnt ask for this. evrything just
happened to me and ther was nothing i
could do."

He never wrote again. Jessie and his workmates
sometimes mentioned him, joked that he murdered
a guard, stole his uniform, and now lived a peaceful
suburban existence.

The letters stuck with Jessie. The rhythm of them,
the palpability of the terrorized mind behind them, as
real as blank white faces that track you in the dark.

*****

At Harvard they dreamt the Clownsquad—an urban terrorist organization under central command, the sole purpose of which was to disrupt people's lives in utterly random fashions. Dressed in clownsuits, they might hose you down on your way to work, toilet paper your car at the parking meter, shove a pie in your face during the board meeting. Worse, when ordered, you'd be forced to wear the dreaded Dogmask, a child's mask attached with a rubber band, which you could not remove for twenty-four hours. Newscaster Senator, TV host, you MUST wear the DOGMASK.

You'd never know when or where The Clownsquad might strike. On the office commode you'd have the door flung open and all your employees watching you. You'd never know. Humiliation might strike at any time, any place, day or night. It would keep you on edge, they decided, bring you down a few notches, destroy this illusion of predictability we've conjured about the lives we lead, dismiss the notion that this earth is a safe and comfortable place.

If you care to know how we think, we, *us*—
Negroes—read your Shakespeare. The basics, "Romeo
and Juliet," "A Midsummer Night's Dream," "King Lear,
"Macbeth," then listen. Somewhere, far off in the
distance you'll hear Ellington. "Such Sweet Thunder."
Othello's tragedy gets its tongue surgically glued to
its cheek, and here, Romeo's romance sways with the
sweetest sadness, a melody the beauty of which can
barely be borne, and you cry just thinking about, for
everything you've ever wanted and never got, or had
and lost. What to say of Hodges? He had a tone like
no other. He uttered profundities grander than those
in any language. There were scars in his sound. But
despite them there was . . . what would you call it? It
wasn't a smile. It wasn't a cry. Something in between—a
clown dancing the waltz while a tear sears his mask.
It's the smile he wears for the audience. The smile
they demand; and quite frankly, anything this horribly
sad must have it. That's the difference. While white
western romantics wear their hearts on their sleeves,
the bloodier the better, we are . . . what? Too wise? Too

proud? Too wise to think our little selves deserve the bombast and fanfares, or too proud to let you see us cry? Who knows. What matters is, we so often end with that shrug of the shoulders, with pride masking the pain. We often end with that reluctant and profoundly, devastatingly acquiescent, "Oh, well."

Chapter XIV

GODS

He wasted no time. After graduation, he barely set foot in Grandier's house before he hopped on a plane for Los Angeles, a couple of screenplays under his arm, ready to make his name. Harvard had files on alumni working in various industries. Jessie scoured the film files and wrote letters, securing several appointments.

He was thrilled to get a meeting with Jerry Rosenblatt, of the talent agency of Honors, Baum and Rosenblatt, supposedly among the most reputable and powerful literary agents in town. He donned an inappropriate light blue suit and headed to Beverly Hills, ascended to the penthouse and stepped into a spacious lobby, where he was immediately overcome by the desire to pee.

Sitting in the glass-enclosed penthouse lobby, the brown smoggy skies staring back through the windows, Jessie's urge to pee remained even after he'd done the deed. A babbling brook ran through the lobby, real water running through a plant-lined marble course as if through a wood. He expected little porcelain frogs and perhaps a plastic elf or two. It was the tackiest thing he had ever seen.

The secretary arrived to sweep him into Rosenblatt's office. He felt awkward and young, as if playing grown-up, his unease congealing into belligerence as, in his heart, he knew his act to be shabby and weak.

Between phone calls from clients demanding that person X had to be fired and complaining that $1,000 a day just wasn't sufficient per diem, Rosenblatt spoke of a script Jessie had submitted.

"Comedy's your thing, I can see that, and that's the hardest thing to do so it's in the most demand. I had a client, a couple o' clients, a team, starving to death six months ago and now they got a network deal worth half a million, so it happens. I could farm you out to a TV outfit, get you going that way while you did the features on the side. I could see you pulling down 250, half a million a script down the line. You think being black's gonna hold you back? It won't, lemme tell you. They won't care if you're green as long as you can write . . ."

He went on and on like this, the phone ringing, his secretary's disembodied voice booming, "so and so on the line."

"Excuse me," he said, "Gotta take this." Talking too loud for four or five minutes and starting up again with, "Where was I . . .?" throughout all of which Jessie sat in stunned, silent disgust, feeling the muscles in his face constrict, involuntarily, like rigor mortis, into a pre-nauseous scowl.

"Where was I . . .?" Rosenblatt hung up the phone. "Yeah. You think Lear has black writers workin' all those shows? No way. Just the on-camera talent, I tell you. He just exploits the on-camera talent. Everyone's not like that. They don't all make such a big deal about how big and different and liberal they are when they're just makin' a buck. Yeah. I can see a year or two from now, gettin' you into features. 250, 500 a pop."

Jessie said nothing. He listened. He watched this silver-haired man with the impeccably groomed air sitting behind an enormous marble desk with the silver lamp's pencil-neck arcing from one end of the huge room to another . . . Jessie watched his lips move and listened to words that made no sense to him. It couldn't be real, he knew. He assumed it was all lies and so labeled this man cruel. Offensive and cruel. It had to be lies because this man had to see that he did not know what to do . . . how to respond . . . how to *be*. He had to see that he was not whole, but he spoke words of hope and encouragement anyway. Cruel. So Jessie smoked furiously and spoke, all told, four words, all at once, at the end of the meeting, while staring at a large glass object on the huge desk in front of him; and unbeknownst to him, in doing so discarded an opportunity he hadn't the wisdom or cynicism to recognize as both rare and golden, and simultaneously self-serving and disingenuous.

"Is this," he asked, "an ashtray?"

*****

To live as Jessie wished to live, a life on film, a life recorded, is the dream of many now. Little children long to be vengefully famous and rich, their videos shared and their lives dissected by countless strangers. Without gods, there are few other ways, and none as simple and demandless, to make this life bearable. Under the camera's watchful eye, even the random writhings of artlessly composed days appear significant compared to those endured in obscurity. That's why Jessie turned to film. He dreamt at least his surrogate self up there, vainly immortalized. The hurts and stings of his youth and beyond would be avenged. He would be better than all of those who'd made him grieve. He never dreamt that one day he would work not because he longed to prove himself better than most, but because he acknowledged his kinship to them . . . that artists weren't artists because they were grander, but because they were so much like so many. For now, though, like so many, he was lonely and sad and needed to be so much more.

*****

The Works sat halfway across town from Jessie's

Beverly Hills-adjacent digs and the bars he frequented. This was a first, but he wasn't as nervous as he had been heading to that first New York waterfront bar. He had been wounded, you see, since then. He was older and a little more desperate.

He parked in the adjacent parking structure and walked briskly, head hung low, afraid of being seen entering the place. Once inside, he faced an alcove with a ticket booth, much like those in movie theatres. There was a menu on a black pinboard. Rooms cost so much, lockers this much less, and condiments (i.e., lubricants, inhalants, and prophylactics) could be had for such and such a price.

Once you paid your money, the buzzer sounded and you passed through the door. Inside, there was a bar-like structure to the side, behind which sat an industrial washer and dryer. Two shirtless men dispensed fresh white towels.

Jessie crossed the beige tiled floor to the locker area. Semi-gothic rock 'n' roll oozed from hidden speakers, and Jessie immediately felt like he had breached an invisible curtain. He had entered another world, one unlike any he had known. He felt exhilarated and mortified as a naked man walked past. He tried not to watch the man's not-quite-flaccid penis bounce up and down. Jessie quickly turned his head so not to meet the stranger's eyes or be caught staring. Once the stranger passed, though, Jessie took a look, and quickly regretted not seeing more because the skin was smooth and the butt round, firm, and downy.

Jessie sat on a long bench between the sets of lockers. He stripped down to his underwear. He listened to the music bounce off the tile and the steady shsshshhshh of water streams hissing through shower nozzles, first one, then more, then fewer then, occasionally, none, as men jumped in and out of showers and filed past the lockers for fresh linens.

Jessie ripped off his underwear and whipped the towel around himself, practically eliminating his nudity. He walked past the lockers to look around.

The showerheads poked from thick, floor-to-ceiling steel rods in the wet area, four per rod. Naked men soaped and rinsed beneath them. Two stood together. The older one soaped down the younger in what looked like a newfound intimacy. Off to the side, the greenish hot tub bubbled and burbled loudly. The smell of chlorine rose with its hot mist. A door near the hot tub opened, and huge white clouds billowed forth and slowly dispersed as nude men emerged all shiny from the steam room.

Turning, Jessie walked down a corridor. Once he got twenty feet from the well-lit showers, it grew dark. Not pitch, but vague and moody. The comfortably familiar shower noise faded and in the bluish dark, he faced a door-lined corridor.

He walked past open doorways to private rooms, cubicles the size of large walk-ins that held long single beds, a large mirror on the opposite wall, and nothing else. Some men leaned naked on the doorposts, like imitation Dietrichs. Some lay on their beds with hands behind their necks, watching the passersby. They waited for the one who would stop and stare, the one whose stare he would return and, with a flick of the head or a smile, invite inside.

A flickering lured Jessie to a room in which men sat on deep, carpeted steps. They stared at porn on a huge video screen. There were newer, quasi-verite, direct-to-videotape for that "U are there look" tapes full of smooth-skinned, dispassionate pretty boys with well-styled hair, or the older, filmed ones in which handsome, muscly older men licked and sucked each other with the abandon of drunks, all to the fuzzy, tacked-on sounds of foolish disco music.

Few spoke loudly here. The hush hung heavy. When loud jockish or nervous, girlish boys came and giggled, they violated something—exactly what, Jessie didn't know, but he knew the sounds of the world shouldn't be here. Perhaps you had to feel alone. Completely; that you had shed the world, the parents and straights who would disapprove. None of them existed here. In here, men of like sex could just *be* . . . Sad to think they had to build a bubble, hermetically sealed, in which to do it, but they'd never do it in the world if they couldn't do it here. Jessie couldn't do it in the world. He could still hear her voice. "I'd kill any son of mine who was queer."

And so in this hushed, shadowy place he turned a corner and saw a tall man, a handsome man, who looked hard at him and touched his skin. Jessie returned the touch, exploratory, tender, and the man looked in Jessie's eyes and smiled. He touched Jessie's face, then kissed him and held him until they stood nude in this darkened hallway, entwined and kissing, as if the need to touch another man had exploded inside each of them. Right there, in the open, they fell on their knees to taste erections, skin of faces brushed against the soft skin of testicles, lips on the velvety skin of inner thighs, hands wrapped around calves and tongues touched everything, fingers and eyelids and arms. Here, they could be all men to each other. Each an iconographic Man to the other, symbols of what they hoped to someday love and be loved by to each other.

Jessie met Tony here. In the steam room, Jessie sat on a bench. Tony spied him and stood in front of him, naked. There was the touching, the steam and the sweat. Tony laid him down and looked in his eyes and filled his mouth with his tongue, all wild and tender like frescoes and statues and all the things that froze desire and want, like the pictures of gods' ecstasies. They came in spasms and shudders with goosebumps on their skin despite the steam and stifling heat.

"Remember how we met?" Tony always said.

Tony had an older lover. They'd been together for many years. Tony and Jessie would see each other at The Works, an unspoken appointment every other Monday night. They'd fuck and then lay naked on a bed and talk for hours. Tony was cocky as hell, but bright and in his straining for abandon, both annoying and magnetic. You could tell it had been easy for him.

Everything. Whether he was lucky, or simply trod the path of least resistance, Jessie never knew.

He had come to LA in the '70s to be gay and wild and free and had hooked up with the lover ten years older who was already a Somebody on the artistic side of the LA actor/theatre scene. Tony knew he was a catch and so latched onto him, and maybe even loved him. He was introduced to the famous Artists in the hills, to the Actresses in the flatlands, where the prettiest men were kept for amusement, who in turn bragged about who'd had whom the nights before.

Gay and pretty, Tony'd found a world where such men were prized, and he took pride in being so prized. They were all young and gorgeous and money was easy, the living cheap, and the sweet scent of endless, brass-ring possibilities blanketed everything like the dark of an eclipse.

As if the tale encapsulated his world, Tony told him about Rick, who, between June 21 and September 21, removed his shirt if the sun shone, regardless of the temperature. Living in Los Angeles, Rick considered doing so his right as a beautiful man. His chest stood broad and firm and browned by the sun, sharp stark lines between the rounded muscles. The shoulders sat equally broad and sculpted and his waist was small, the stomach taut and chiseled. He worked out every day. Sit-ups, push-ups, squats, free weights, at a local gym known for producing beautiful men. He shaved clean his chest and legs so the muscles shimmered, lightly oiled, so that he glowed, hard and smooth and golden.

Sweat poured down Rick's chest the night he met Tony. The Laguna Beach night had never cooled. The air stayed warm, with the sea breeze just a wisp of its normal night-brisk self. Inside, Rick and a hundred others danced to music so loud their hearts beat in sync with the bass. Most had their shirts off and even in this company Rick shone, his form cleaner, broader, or slimmer whenever needed, as if it gauged the competition and instantaneously altered itself to compensate. Sweat glistened on his perfect skin and his short hair, thoroughly wet, clumped together in thick communal shafts, like a porcupine's spikes.

Men watched him dance. Years ago, he watched and liked the ones whose hips and stomachs thrust with the beat. He liked the ones who unhooked the top buttons on their jeans, so you took hints of the silky, loosely haired flesh below the belt line. Now he danced like them and the sweat poured all the way down to his opened jeans wetting the downy hair below.

The floor was packed. Each move brought his wet skin in touch with other warm flesh. The boy he danced with moved closer. The boy had been been staring at Rick all night and when the boy finally asked him to dance, he agreed. Seeing the boy's want, Rick humored him. He moved closer, put his hands on the boy's waist so that their bodies touched. He felt the boy's erection through his jeans. Rick looked down and gave him one of those looks, those "ooh yeah" sex-looks, with the misty eyes and the head tossed back in a study of mild ecstasy as the boy ground his crotch deeper into his own.

Tony danced nearby. The boy didn't know that Rick was eyeing someone else. Tony knew, though. He felt it. With his long black hair and clean-shaven babyface, he didn't look like the others. The hair gave him a counter-cultural air, while his eyes said sex longer and louder than all the bumpings and grindings around him. The tall slim frame he owned, lived in, seemed a part of him while the gym-muscled bodies surrounding it all looked like knight's armor, grafted on, uncomfortable gowns worn to impress.

To make his unfaithful older lover jealous, Tony had planned to pick up the hottest man in the bar, and Rick was it.

Twelve years later, gray littering his jet black hair, crow's feet engraving the skin around his still beautiful eyes, Tony told Jessie, "You should have seen my lover's face when he saw me with Rick. He almost fainted. I just said to him, 'how you doin'?' as we passed and kept walking. Rick was the hottest guy in the bar and that's what I said I'd get. And I did. It was easy though. I was pretty. Even after that, after Rick knew I had a lover, we stayed friends. We liked to pal around together. We were both pretty."

It was these who were the most devastated. They'd found what they'd been looking for—thirsts slaked, needs met, wants indulged—which eventually became their curse because they didn't want enough; and who would have dreamt that so small a crime could wreak such bloody havoc.

So many died quickly. The ones who wanted fun, who'd stare out from the terrace of a rich man's Laguna Beach home to boast, "I've had every good-looking guy on this beach." The ones who stayed up all night dancing and drinking, with drugs of the moment close at hand, so goddamned needy that they had to stay and strut as long as men were there to watch and want them, who had been so bruised and hurt and torn that those vulgar attentions became like food and air, that they would give themselves to almost any man who asked.

"I mean it," one said to Jessie, one who knew he was ill and would probably die. "If I can't be like I've been and do what I've done, I don't want to live."

Those died quickly, and later, slowly, over years, others, some like-minded, others shut-ins or neurotics almost too scared to touch anything, no rhyme or reason to any of it. All of them innocents. The wildest of them probably the most so.

Rick died, beautiful Rick, then years later Tony's lover died. In between more friends, and more and more until Tony stood alone at the top of the hill, in a house bought years ago when land was cheap so he and his lover and all their friends could look down on the world beneath them, like Gods.

Chapter XV

THE ALCOHOLICS

A Bud bottle slapped down in front of him. The bartender looked like Big Bird: a hooked nose, tall, blond hair and glasses. Despite the fact that, feature for feature, he wasn't stuff of fantasy, he managed sexy through sloppy grace and looseness, his fuck-em-if-they-can't-take-a-joke honesty. Jessie sat on a stool at this video bar, staring at the big screen when the bartender propped his elbows on the bar, laid his head in the cup of his hands and said, "You wanna go out with me?" Jessie's response ("Not really") marked the beginning of a friendship. That's the way they started, a chance remark, a shared laugh at someone or something nearby. You'd run into him again, whoever he was. Here in Beverly Hills Adjacent, the two or three bars saw every face in town in the course of a week, 75% on Saturday night alone.

That's how he met Cliff.

An acquaintance introduced them. Cliff stood in the bar with his hands in his khaki pants pockets, preppie striped button-down, his topsider-shod feet sockless. His head perched on his neck like a hawk's and, while his jaw worked the gum he chewed, he looked both scared and mean. He spoke with a lazy drawl, the shoulders often bouncing up and down after his own witticisms.

They stood abreast in a bar when the man who introduced them went for drinks.

"So what brings you out here tonight?" Cliff drawled disinterestedly.

"The cotillion got rained out," Jessie drawled back, a little pissed.

"I hate it when that happens," Cliff replied, cracking a smile. "Wet crinoline smells really bad."

"I had a place at the Baccarat tables, but Monaco's gotten impossibly tacky since Grace died."

"There's nothing worse than a soggy cotillion and a tacky duchy. So you came to a gay bar instead."

"You try getting laid in wet, smelly taffeta."

Set 'em up; knock 'em down. With each other they indulged themselves, being as obtuse or as gross as they pleased, knowing the other could match it or better. They soon called each other before going out, meeting up and hanging out. They called each other at work to gossip or read perverse items from the morning paper. They spoke or saw each other every day. They became the best of friends.

Cliff introduced him to some interesting folk—a bright bunch of gay alcoholics. Jessie hadn't met anyone like them since school. For the first time in this burg he was having some fun.

They'd talk about anything. Say anything. Rusty, tall, thin, and swishy, hunted a big strong man to call his own. He'd toned himself down from silver lamé pants and lipstick to no-makeup and skin-tight jeans. He considered this great progress. "Girlfriend, I wouldn't leave the house without full makeup. I used to vacuum with my shirttails tied at the midriff, just like Laura Petrie." He'd never heard such humiliating detail so entertainingly packaged. Another of them talked about the days he spent in a care unit, straight-jacketed and baying at the moon. They talked about what messes they were, but Jessie didn't see it. They seemed so much like himself. Thus, they eyed each other knowingly and uttered sayings like, "We'll save you a seat," which referred to AA meetings, suggesting he would succumb to booze. With a father like Grandier, Jessie disliked liquor. He drank wine with special dinners, but that was all. Their cocky assurance remained, however, and he paid them no mind.

They took him to an AA meeting. When someone said "Hi, I'm so and so and I'm an alcoholic" and everybody screamed "HI SO-AND-SO" he almost jumped out of his skin. If anyone so-much-as belched, they all burst into applause. A speaker took the lectern and launched into a pert-near professional stand-up bit, very funny, occasionally touching or thought provoking, all in all, high comedy. At the end, they passed a basket, said a prayer, and went home. It was much cheaper than a night at a club. He understood why these folks attended so regularly.

When Jessie and Cliff went to bars together, each kept an eye out for the other's "type." They'd watch each other pick up men, encourage each other to do so, Jessie especially, egging Cliff on. He'd call the next day for the rundown, always glad to hear the catastrophic details—that Cliff couldn't get it up or the guy puked in his bed.

After the shit had hit the fan, Rusty said, "That's the part I don't get. How could you watch him go with other guys all the time, even push him on them?"

Jessie didn't know what it felt like. He'd never done it before. He was young. He'd never believed in it. As he had with moonlight, he considered it a fiction, or a sickness. He remembered the tears Lulene shed upon deciding to leave Grandier and being told she cried because "She loves him." He remembered her on her knees methodically shredding his pictures. He remembered watching Grandier, scotch in hand, TV in the background, tearily saying, "No matter what you saw . . . You don't know what wen' on behind closed doors. Your mama loved me."

He couldn't believe in it. It didn't exist. The depictions he had seen were either insipid, like the ones on TV and in bad movies, or, more to his liking, murderous and tragic like in the films noir. He was alone. He always had been and, he assumed, always would be. To the fallacy—the myth of love—he felt immune. It was just another something, like booze or dope or Jesus Christ, that people used to drag themselves through another useless, Godless day.

So he could never remember when he realized he loved him, that he would ache to see him, above all others, to tell him something good, to seek his approval, above all others, his good wishes and congratulations, above all others. Jessie loved Cliff, and he did not know what to do.

"OH MY GOD," Rusty howled when Jessie told him. He was begging for clues of a reciprocity that Rusty couldn't offer.

He just had to tell Cliff. Having admitted this much, he couldn't go back to how it was. He tried avoiding him, but that didn't work. He had to say it.

And so, one evening, when the group sat at a coffee shop, he took Cliff around the corner, stood him up against a brick wall near the dumpster in the alley, and for the first time since he was twelve, told another human being that he loved him.

Cliff stood silent, once Jessie'd clarified the difference between "love" which Cliff heartily professed, and "in love" which left him speechless. His piece spoken, Jessie turned and walked away. Thinking back, he couldn't pin down his expectations. An "I've been dying to say the same to you, my sweet . . ." with open arms or a "Eeeeeuuccgggghhhh." He couldn't remember wanting or expecting either. In a way, he walked right into it, like holding your hand over an open flame, like putting the burning end of a cigarette to your own flesh. He walked into it.

Jessie cried a lot the next few days. He refused to speak to Cliff when he called. He'd ask Rusty for news of him, but Rusty wisely refused the role of middleman. Jessie just ached. He made up a line. Cliff was white and he told Cliff's friends that he couldn't have a white boyfriend. A white one, a male one, he just couldn't have one.

Such things were not for him. He stood above them and wallowed beneath them. They occupied the human realm from which he stood apart, by design, by nature, by whose fault? So he cried for what he could not have, for what he had tasted and would rather have cut out his tongue than taste any more.

That's how Jessie fell in love.

*

Something ached after Cliff. Jessie felt the ache without recognizing it was there. It was such a subtle shift from his usual fear and longing. He later thought it funny that love for a drunk turned him into one, but that was the case. After Cliff, what he used to take or leave without a thought weighed more heavily. The men he would eye, too scared to approach, the thoughts of them, the wants and needs, they all meant more.

He had trouble sleeping. He tried everything. He went to the doctor thinking he had a tumor sitting on his brain's sleep center but the doctor told him there were no physical causes. He drank warm milk and ate big meals before bedtime but that solved nothing.

Yearning kept him up at night. For what, he didn't know—save for everything he did not have and feared he never would. This was new, and he tossed and turned wondering what would end it. Warm flesh? Men's arms? Renown?

To shop a screenplay full of white characters, he procured a Hollywood agent with a notable outfit, a half-black, half-Jewish woman with a lazy, sensual air who dressed kinda slutty only to shock you with a quick, sharp mind. He "took" meetings, white producers' mouths dropping when a black face filled their doorways.

He needed money. He reduced it to that. Simple. Tangible. He needed a success to prove—to Grandier, his sisters, that dead woman—to all of them what he was worth. He would show them. He needed the money a triumph would bring to prove them wrong. He needed it to feel like someone. Grandier's "a black man gotta be twice as good as a white one . . ." and Lulene's "you're nothing if you're black and poor . . ." both the progeny of the spit of white men—had done their work so well.

But that chance grew more dim. A brief success, some money paid, and then nothing, no more meetings, no "maybes"; no more possibilities. He wrote more, other scripts, but they received less interest. No commission offers came, no rewrite jobs, nothing.

One night, leftover wine lulled him to sleep without a thought; without a worry. He reached that brief oblivion, effortlessly. It felt more welcoming that anything in a long time.

There was a way home.

Several nights a week he spent in bars and discos, some alone, some with friends, having fun sometimes, others alone, watching, waiting, for the smile, the look in the eyes, the carriage that would mean interest, the look of someone whom he could love, and could love him, a look he never saw, or if he did, could not recognize, and if he recognized, feared too much.

So, each night, he headed on home.

Chapter XVI

MING

For his wife, David Murray wrote a song that the World Saxophone Quartet performed. Murray's solo opens it, searching wildly, reining in, desperate for control in the midst of having none, and then the other horns enshrine the melody; full of awe—disbelief—that joy so deep; it melts into something worse than sadness.

You can barely stand to lie there with him in your arms when after all this time you found him and he makes you laugh and loves you, knows you, and you want to take care of him forever. Hold him and love him forever. He had yearned for someone to love him a song as sweet as those horns sang, and now he finally found that one man to whom an invisible cord tethered him like an umbilicus, he understood why all those songs and works he had worshipped seemed so sad—that to love meant seeing death—an ending because this love would end one way or another—seeing it as clearly as light and saying hello, shaking hands, and laying down with it, to sleep at night, a blanket of death for you and someone you'd kill for, to keep from harm—your home . . . your heart . . . your eyes . . . lips . . . blood.

DELIRIUM TREMENS

The apartment gleamed more brightly than ever. He'd cleaned up from the two weeks he had spent holed up in there, lying in the bed, TV remote control in hand and a bottle of vodka nearby. He'd washed the floors and shampooed the carpet, thrown away countless empty liquor bottles and thrown away or washed and dried the clothes and bedthings he had vomited on, night after night.

All was spotless. Three days ago he had called some friends and told them what he had only told himself—only admitted staring bleary-eyed at his morning face, the one with the bruise-like circles under the eyes, and saying to his reflection, "You . . . are an alcoholic." Three days ago told them what had happened and he dragged himself to their house where he stayed for three days, during which time he could not eat or sleep, having made the decision to stay alive amidst the drinking that ravaged his body to the point of killing it, little knowing that the next phase would savage his mind.

Sober now, back at his own apartment, he had cleaned it all up. No trace remained of the bottles and the mess. He could eat now, and slept some. The sweat still poured. He couldn't stop that, and his hands still shook, nothing like they had before—not those enormous quakes from before. He could stand and hold things now.

He felt good, strangely giddy. Happy thoughts swam through his head. That morning, he was sure there would be a party. The skies above lay clear and blue, and a pleasant wind whooshed up and down the tree-lined street outside the church where he waited for a friend to pick him up from an AA meeting. His second. All the radios of all the cars whizzing up and down the street blared the same song: The Replacements "Shooting Dirty Pool." The same cars kept driving back and forth, up and down. All the people inside them stared at him. Grand. Enormous. His friends had dragged everyone in on it. Cars with streamers drove up and down the street playing songs he loved—a bright parade just for him. On the way home, he dropped hints, hints that he knew of the grand plot his friends had hatched, but he never let on. His friend never admitted they had planned a party for him.

Back at his apartment, he giggled endlessly, waiting, knowing that at any time "SURPRISE" would sound and bodies would pop up to cheer him. He started to vacuum, a final pass before the festivities. He giggled even more. He couldn't believe it. He turned the vacuum on and off, two or three times because it was just so goddamned ingenious. The machine itself played that same song in a little music box drone. They'd rigged the vacuum cleaner as part of the set-up. He laughed and laughed, loving it. His friend left—to put the plan in action, he knew.

As evening fell, he heard the music from one of the rock clubs on the Sunset Strip, as if the song he had heard all day transmorgrified into a live band playing. It must have been a special concert. He could never hear the music from his house before. They must have put speakers outside the club. The celebratory air spilled down from Sunset Boulevard. Crowded House played; bad-boy troubadours playing endless variations on "Now We're Getting Somewhere," serving it up in everything from waltz time to samba. He kept wanting to go take a look but never did. The edges seemed too sharp, the colors too bright here in his own room, like a cartoon come to life, and he couldn't quite bring himself to leave.

Laying on his bed, he dozed a few moments and woke to the tiny tingling of something crawling on his skin. With a start, he woke and brushed his leg. Sitting up, he took stock, assuring himself the thing was off him. Then he felt more. More. All over. He couldn't shake them off. Spiders. Tiny black spiders. Lethal. He remembered the skill he had learned, the web spinning he used to perform for pay, circus pay, when people came to see him spin the web from hand to hand containing the tiny lethal creatures, that death defying stunt he knew so well. Standing in the shower, he began the silent ritual. Hand over hand, over thumb and under pinkie he carefully wrapped the silky web thread, the little black spiders dotting it like beads, one bite from any of which, the tiniest scratch from any of which meant death.

Terrified, his arms and hands flew before him in elaborate circles as the shower water rained down. His whole being tensed to make every move smooth and precise. He didn't want to die, not in agony, not from the bite of one of these—and not alone. The fear, the panic unlike any he had known, save in nightmares, made him falter, his elegant hand motions jerky and clumsy, and the web, the ever-lengthening web grown beyond his control, clinging to his naked flesh despite the water falling all around.

He thought he might still recover, but he couldn't. His hands flew faster but the web kept growing and the little black spiders fell all around him. He dove from the shower, panting and breathless, his legs and hands pumping furiously to brush the things from his skin, pounding them off of him, smashing them underfoot. He grabbed the clippers and fumbled with the cord until he plugged it in and heard the bbbzzzzzzzz. With shaking hands he laid the shears to his head, hair falling down in clumps, hair on which he could see the deadly little spiders. Tears streamed down his face as he looked in the mirror, his head nearly shaven, odd little clumps of hair here and there. Almost safe, he threw on some pants and ran to the living room which had never looked so small, and he could see the little black dots crawling on the brown carpet. He ran outside, into the stairway. A neighbor came out, and Jessie sat on the stairs and cried on his knees, and then, when he ran into the street, the plot became clear. They wanted him to do it again. They wanted to see him with the bottle to his lips, shaking and puking like he had been, like something not human any more, so he yelled and screamed outside his building, telling them all to go away and leave him alone because no one would drive him back to where he had been.

Sometime during that night, he died. He didn't know exactly when. Time reached out before him like a hand and he could see it laid out as clearly: what had transpired since his death to old friends, Family, John and Sally and Archie. Some had garnered a bit of fame and he saw their pictures in newspaper clippings. He had died, and he was alone in a dark nether-world that looked like his apartment, but wasn't, as if his spirit had dragged the spirits of inanimate things along with it, and those spirits sat all around him without giving any comfort, any warmth, offering nothing familiar, just cold vague replicas, mockeries of living things, like himself.

In the blue-gray fog, he wondered where to go. Seeing the past, not even the past, time, nothing straight and clear but amorphous and random, a snatch here and a piece there, like airborne debris, floating past him like leaves in a warm August wind that he would snatch up, examine, then set free.

He got in the car that night; snuck away, in his underwear, having nothing to wear, knowing it made no difference. He got in his car to find a place for his soul. In one of those snatches of time he saw Family and he thought of finding them. Out there.

As he drove the streets of time, space, images and faces flew past him, streetlights like specters, gravestones, markers of things that had been and were no more. He drove and drove, tinny voices in his ear, as if those snatches of past and future bore non-sync soundtracks, aural montages of people and places he hadn't seen in years, times he had not lived long enough to see.

The night passed. Daylight returned. Where the night had gone, he didn't know, but now, with the sun, the cameras had arrived to film his morning show. Something like "Coffee with Barbara's Mom"—one of those loose, shaggy dog-type morning shows that he hosted from his car. The camera truck mounted on another car followed his, the directional mike pointing at his window as he, newspaper over his lap, commented brightly on the local sights, parts of Los Angeles he had never seen before, a travelogue of sorts, his wit amazing even him. Gales of laughter filled his car as he made his way nowhere in particular, as one car among thousands on Los Angeles roadways contained a dead man in his underwear, hosting a local morning talk show.

✳✳✳✳✳

He remembered the ride in the police car. He remembered sitting in the back of the car in his underwear, the two cops in front, his hands cuffed behind his back. They asked his name and he did not know it.

After a long car ride, the view during which he enjoyed, although he found the cuffs a bit uncomfortable, he was lifted and jostled and landed handcuffed to something in an empty room.

It took him a while to appreciate the cunning. Sitting there, in his underwear, in this bare room, his hands cuffed behind him to a horse. They had attached to his wrists these razor-sharp cuffs of which he'd heard tell. Infernal things, really. The more he struggled, the tighter they grew, the sharp edges cutting deeper and deeper into the flesh, and then the bone, until ultimately, severing the hands altogether. He hoped they'd cut the arteries fast enough that he would lose consciousness; but they'd thought of that, and once past a certain point the evil steel did its work quickly, so, while the sweet red juices pumped steadily to waste in pools around you, you never missed the agony of bone crushed and mangled.

He wondered about the horse likewise rigged. What crime it had committed, steel-trapped to a man condemned, whinnying and naying, and worse, shitting in horror?

He concentrated all his will on sitting still, and, all told, the horse behaved well, sitting motionless behind him; though, with its diarrhea, the stench became overwhelming as the warm, steamy fluid spurted out from under it. Writhing against the stench, he felt the cuffs tighten. He heard the metallic click as they clenched one notch tighter and he wriggled against the smell and warmth of the horse filth all around him. He knew he'd need a song. That would set the rhythm, and then, gently, he would coax the horse to follow, to sway oh so gently, to the song's irresistable measure.

Home no more home to me,
whither must I wander?
Hunger my driver I go where I must.
Cold blows the winter wind over hill and heather:
Thick drives the rain and my roof is in the dust.

The melody soothed him. Gently, he rocked his body back and forth and felt the horse sway with him. To encourage the horse, he farted in time. The horse responded so well, its expurgations spewing in time to his song, the merry air making even that foul brew smell sweet. He too, feeling overwhelmed with the vision of winning his freedom, felt the warm expulsion under him, the steamy lubricant mashed beneath his buttocks as he rocked back and forth, hearing the cuffs click mechanically, but feeling their grip loosen, not grasp. Man and beast united in song and good feeling, rocking to freedom in their small cell.

DRINKING

The TV network layoff had come a few months ago with a check for five grand, and he decided, while looking for another job, to write. He worked long and hard. But the nights got longer and harder, too. Jobless, money running out, nights became fearsome things, each hour of the day like seconds on a detonator, the minutes before explosion, when he had to face the night and the fears that lunged at him like ghouls. So during the day he sat at his Macintosh, writing about murders, betrayals, manipulative fathers and murderous, self-loathing sons, feeling the scowl burn into his features as he wrote, the hate pouring into his terminal but freeing him from nothing.

At night, he tried all the time. He'd lay down to bed with no liquor in the house, begging and pleading to fall to sleep but instead fighting all the usual vultures, pecking and clawing. So he gave in. He got up and went to the corner liquor store to get the bottle and poured a tumbler-full, climbed back into bed, and sipped, straight, until he slipped into the only peace he knew.

He remembered the time, the moment. Sitting at his computer, at his desk with a grimace contorting his face as he wrote. Just as he finished, typed in the part in which one man asks what kind of hell it was he had come to, and another answers, "It's my home," he realized this was real. There was no future time that he could pick like a suit of clothes at which his life would begin. He could not flick the "on" switch upon attaining fame or money or the love he dreamt would follow those. It *was* and it continued, even now. Even sitting there at this desk, the moments passed inexorably, one hopeless second after another, never to be retrieved or redeemed, one hopeless hungover second after another and he didn't think he could bear it—the thought of that time, whole years. Years in jobs he loathed with no one near him, years of waiting and hoping and getting nothing for it, of anger, of hating what they'd done to him and missing someone. Missing someone. Years and hates came tumbling back on him like explosions in films going backwards, debris falling back on him, a whole life's worth of debris, and that twenty-eight years could spread such mess repulsed him. He realized that this was his life, this mess, not the rosy future he had planned, nor the tomorrows he had promised himself, but what had been and what was, this hell in which he spent each night running from dogs that would tear him apart if it weren't for that clear juice that silenced them.

So he took more of it. More. Straight from the bottle in large gulps knowing he couldn't stand these thoughts much longer, longing to feel nothing, know nothing; until he woke again, dark outside, and he stumbled to the living room to find that bottle again because the moment his eyes could see, they saw ugliness, and he couldn't stand it. So he drank more and knew and felt nothing until he could see and then drank more again so he would see nothing.

*****

Rushing to the bathroom to vomit for the thousandth time, banging into door jambs and falling over things, his body covered with black and purple bruises now, finally his legs crumbled beneath him and his whole body shook. He tried to stand but his legs collapsed. They wobbled like an ancient man's. His heart pounded as fiercely as his arms and hands trembled. His body was not his and he knew who owned it now—death owned it. He hadn't wanted this. Oblivion he would have welcomed, hoping for another chance, in some rosier time, just a respite until the coming of a world in which he would have his place. But Jessie did not want to die.

And so, foot by foot, he crawled—because he could not make his quaking limbs obey enough to walk—to the telephone, and told a friend what he had only told a mirror, and he went there, where he lay for several days, perpetually awake, trying to sleep but his eyes twitching back and forth beneath his closed eyelids and fantastical, phantasmagoric images flashing through his mind until he thought himself okay, took himself home to succumb completely to the visions in his head; to die; and wander the streets desperate for a place a dead man might call home.

*

They had asked him to demonstrate. God. He couldn't remember how long ago that was. Ages, as if he had grown old lying here, in his underwear, strapped to this bed in this cavernous gray room, even the sun-rays slanting through the windows shining gray, a room double-lined with beds like his, and men like him, strapped, silent and helpless.

Their idea of a joke, he supposed. To lay him there, strap him down, then leave. He thought his fellow actors in this film would be right back to rescue him, but they never came, and then the crew, the grips, the lights, the set folk, all left, leaving him alone there, strapped to that bed. He yelled and screamed and thrashed, but doctors and nurses paid him no mind. They assumed he was just another screaming patient.

That was years ago, and every day since, when the nurses came and held the little plastic bottle under his dick, which had been trained to pee when so handled, every day he tried to tell them they'd made a mistake. But they wouldn't listen. The drugs made time fade as if in dreams, float, waft, so swiftly and sparklingly it took his breath away. He didn't know if he imagined it, but he thought they had returned, some year, some time past. They stood at the foot of the bed, she elegant, as always in the large black hat which draped like the wing of a bird over one eye and the tailored suit, some sharp colors slashing through each other like foes; and he, a tailor's dummy, right beside her. They stared at him, triumph and evil in their eyes. What had he done to them? He knew the answer to that. Nothing. Evil. That's all it was. The evil in them. To leave him here in this gray place, stripped and strapped, nothing in each day but fading in and out, watching the shows on the ceilings, when the ventilator slats became like mouths and talked and danced in colorful productions, exhausting him with their antics; nothing to fill the days except the hum of silence, with those who came to violate him almost welcome, their actions like his only friends after so long—to shove his dick in a bottle or, daily, to feel the arm beneath his legs lift them, the warm cloths wipe between his legs, the cold touch of the pan to his flesh . . . as time drifts on, endless, the terror having passed, his first days spent in a horror the likes of which stuck him like knives, the times he woke and couldn't scream, the horror of knowing it wasn't a joke and they weren't coming back, and it wouldn't end and he would be here . . . forever . . . until the terror became this dark gray beauty, as time drifted, and he learned to watch it waft past, and he lay immobile, floating, riding the back of the world like a sleepy boy on a raft . . .

CRYING

The thick black fur made her seem fat and sassy, but petting her, you felt the bones poking through. She was dying. Talia had adopted her in New York, and when she moved to Illinois with her husband, she brought the cat with her.

Predictably, the dying cat Maggie touched Jessie.

Somewhere during his delirium, he called both his sisters and raved semi-coherently about having come back to life, some people breaking down his door to beat him senseless, and other such. When he disappeared for several days, Talia became alarmed and flew her pregnant self to LA.

Jessie woke in a hospital, woozy and strange. He remembered his name and other pertinent details, so they unstrapped him from the bed. Talia carted his weak, sleepless, trembling carcass to her home, where their sister Janice met them. They had a bit of a reunion. They laughed hysterically at mutually remembered scenes, like the time Grandier beat Janice with the iron, and the time he brandished the gun threatening to kill them all and then himself; the girls later took Jessie to a rehab house, where a staff counselor, having heard the details of his case, insisted he not be allowed beyond the four walls for thirty days lest he drink all the liquor—everywere. No, the counselor insisted, he should not sleep the night at Talia's and return the next morning to begin his stay. The demon rum lay in wait.

Thus, he was shown a room, told his sisters would bring his belongings in the morning, and he remained at St. Someone's Drug and Alcohol Rehabilitation Center for the next fortnight.

This particular drunken drama had lost its novelty to Jessie. Having gone through it and survived, it didn't seem as big a deal any more. To him, some barrier had been breached and there was no return to where he had been. To others, however, knowing so little of what had brought him here, there remained the potential for High Drama. He *had* made a mess. Grandiers did not make messes, not public ones that landed them in hospitals strapped to beds like madwomen where strangers might see. To Grandiers, a public mess was unforgivable, and he had laid one great big stinking turd right in the middle of the floor. Immediate incarceration seemed apt.

After two weeks, though, against the doctors orders, having laid a guilt trip on Talia, he assumed outpatient status, taking the bus to the bin daily instead of living there full time. He spent time with Maggie. An odd pair they made, Jessie with the practically bald head (he had shaved it when under spider attack), sitting in a rocker holding this most forlorn of beasts with its greasy fur and the skin-and-bones mien of the dying. The same impulse that had led him to Caesar, the sickly pup, drew him to this dying cat. No one had time to care for it since it lived with a hormonally-imbalanced pregnant woman and a dawn-rising, hard-working man. Jessie sat with her in the rocking chair, and stroked her. He watched her eat, fed her bits from his hand. Despite her age and her frailties, Maggie seemed happy.

Two weeks after he went back home, Talia wrote that Maggie had died. And Jessie finally cried. Great big gasps of grief. He wished he still drank so he could have raised a toast to Maggie. He wished he could have done the same for Gary, for all the ones he had loved and never said goodbye to. That nothing could hurt them anymore. One for the man at the VA. One for Rick and the boys whose names he didn't know. A great big whiskey for Lulene.

do do daaa do do do daaa do do daaaa

"MING"
David Murray

OLD MAN

Grandier sat before his television in his suburban townhouse near Washington, D.C. When his wife was still alive and the kids coming up, there had been a wood across the street, a full block of nothing but tall trees and undergrowth. It was gone now, and apartments stood on the lot, buildings to which he had never grown accustomed. Ten years had gone by. When he walked outside and looked to the right he still expected trees, and those brown buildings insulted him, as if they slapped him with the inexorability of his life's waning and things leaving—their passing him by if he dared step foot outside his door. He didn't leave the house much anymore.

Nothing had changed in here. He'd bought no furniture, changed no rooms, no curtains, no rugs— nothing. When Grandier walked in the living room, the couch still lay covered with the pillows she made; the painting she bought in Germany still hung over it. The Danish modern furniture still sat in the dining room, and behind the glass of the cabinet, the gold leaf plates and cut tinted crystal still sat for show. He had changed nothing.

He hadn't changed the children's rooms. Talia's still had the fake French provincial, bought cheap, white with gold trim, frilly and girlish. Janice's room still bore her malice. She had kept it messy out of spite, knowing every time Grandier looked inside he saw defiance, the heavy dark-wood furniture bespeaking the sheer weight of the contempt she loved to show for him. When he walked past that room, the memory of that contempt hit him. Still.

Jessie's room. He still half expected to see that dog curled up on the bed, its head on the pillow like it thought it was a person, or sitting in that big windowsill looking out and barking at folks walking by. This one hurt the most. The room was on a corner and he couldn't see in; not just from walking by. He was glad of that. He hadn't looked in there in years. The maid wiped the dust away.

His boy. The last one in the whole Grandier family. The last one in the whole world. His boy. He'd jumped for joy when he heard it was a boy. He barely remembered his own father, but he knew what to do. He always read the stories in the paper about fathers and sons, anything to do with them. Stories about them building things together or doing things together. You might say he studied it—fathers and sons—so he knew what to do. And almost from the start, it went wrong. The boy didn't like to touch him. Cried when it was near him. He thought the boy would get used to him so he would hold him while he cried. Just hold him, shushing, assuming he would get used to him and quit his crying—worse come to worse, just get tired and sleep.

He never stopped, turning his little head away, that face so small but all screwed up like it tasted something sour, a face Lulene had when she hated him and he kissed her and tried to make up with her. It was like he inherited that face from her.

She was so pretty. Everyone said so. She made all those Army wives look like hags. They just didn't know. He said his children would never know what went on between them, what happened behind closed doors, but they acted like it didn't matter. They only saw the fights and the cussing. Those kids thought that was all that mattered, that that was all there was.

He thought he was the luckiest man in the world when he walked into that room and saw her lying there, so beautiful, with that beautiful boy in her arms, his little eyes closed, his skin honey and his hair black silk on his head. "This is mine," he thought.

At first, he kept himself busy. Having been in the Army transportation corps, he traveled cheap, so he flew back and forth between New Orleans and Plattville, visiting. In the beginning, he would visit Talia or Janice, or they would come home. He didn't mind if they just came to borrow money or get something they'd left in the house. Jessie never came.

He didn't know how he got here. He didn't know how she died. He couldn't see how he got left sitting in this house full of nothing but old things that reminded him of what he hadn't done, and who hated him, and who would rather have died than go on living here. He didn't know how it had happened.

He would live long. Everyone in his family did. The graying, thinning hair, joints that wouldn't move, heart beating irregular. It wasn't that. It wasn't the body. The spirit . . . whatever you call it. Whatever made him want to go on wasn't there anymore. Whatever joys he took were gone.

He needed some things from the store. He wanted a steak. The doctor told him to stop eating them. He had, almost. He used to have them every night. Now, once every couple of weeks. That was all. He was out of scotch. And that song was still in his head, years since he heard it, on one of Jessie's old records.

No one knows I loved you more
Than I could bear to know

A steak would be nice. He'd broil it rare. He kept the TV tray right there. It didn't matter much what was on. He'd find something funny.

I hurt you
I lied
It's all I could show

He liked the one with the old ladies in it. Especially the grandmother who talked about wetting the bed and her dentures falling out. She broke him up.

But somewhere deep down
I hope that you saw
A shallow glimmer in the haze
That said 'I love you'
Then, now, despite the rage

I will die hurting the hurt you felt
From my broken love for you

Fall settled into winter. Only a few leaves still hung on the trees. Years ago, this time, the streets would have been full of leaves fallen from the trees in the wood across the way. If he looked out the windows, he saw the gray sky. Close to the window, he could feel the cold. He'd make do with what he had in the house. He didn't want to go outside.

Chapter XVII

JUST . . . TIDDY-BOOM

Tony had really pissed him off. Jessie swore he wouldn't call him during this last lull in their years-long on-and-off, and he had kept his word. Tony claimed it was mourning, that he mourned his recently deceased lover, that he'd been away working, avoiding the house they'd shared at the top of the hill, and that now, back home, he mourned. Well, since Jessie now saw him in a cruise bar, he supposed the mourning was over. Tony ran over to him and said, "I haven't heard from you."

Jessie could have spat. This son-of-a-bitch had the gall to bound up to him dressed in a leather vest and nothing else from the waist up saying, "I haven't heard from you," as if in reproach?

"I don't think so."

Jessie'd thought that this time it might come to something. Of late, Tony had seemed a bit less cocky. He seemed older, definitely, and with luck, wiser. Now, death had touched him, which tended to mature one. A year ago Jessie had broken up with Patrick, a thity year-old obsessed with being twenty-one again, an adoptee of now-dead Utah Mormons, the female of which used to dress him up in girls' clothes until he was twelve. David wasn't well. Considering from whence he'd come, Jessie had thought a return to Tony a giant step forward.

Oh, well.

After seething for a few moments, quietly and politely, not willing to give the prick the satisfaction of seeing him pissed, Jessie left and headed to the sleazy/artsy quasi-dive filled with the horniest of the horny where he planned to get laid, and well laid, for spite if nothing else.

On his previous trip to this place, he had seen a normie. The denizens divided neatly into four groups: *Beasts*, as in the purposefully disfigured, the obese, the ring-through-the-nose S&M types, the leathered, the obviously insane; *Leatherbabies*, budding beasts, young and sometimes attractive, but already complete fetishists; *Trendoids*, the crucifix wearing, ugly shoe, Caligula haircut types who collected performance artists and Mexican religious fetish objects; and *Normies*, regular horny folk who got a charge from the place's undeniable sexual energy.

That other night, Jessie spotted a couple of normies, and here, tonight, was one of them. He was cute but needed study. Prior to approaching men in bars, Jessie observed discreetly for lengths of time. He could tell a lot by watching. This one stared back, but showed him little. He didn't stand, so Jessie couldn't see how he walked. He smiled at no one, so Jessie couldn't check his teeth; sitting, Jessie couldn't see his butt; in a crowd so that Jessie couldn't see his shoes. In other words, he gave Jessie no cause to dismiss him, and was not predatorily inclined enough, not enough the trophy man, to hunt Jessie down.

Their first date was uneventful, but on the third, they clicked. A drunk like Jessie, he had been a junkie, too. He emerged from the lows—the needle parks, the filthy rooms—that Jessie had been too falsely proud and rightfully scared to endure. James loved to read but hated highbrow books and insisted jazz gave him diarrhea. He once held out his hand and said to Jessie, "Pull my finger," (which Jessie did) and cut a venomous fart. Jessie was shocked, appalled and thrilled. James punctured that big lead balloon filled with grandiosity, terror, and overcompensatory pride that Jessie had spent a lifetime in the crushing task of hoisting aloft; and he gave Jessie no choice but to let that one thing he had to hold on to crash down to earth. This man whose hand warmed his . . . this man laid Jessie's grand plans to ruin, burned them to the ground, hacked them, trampled them as remorselessly as some animal tears a bloody corpse. Whatever dreams of deathless triumph had nurtured him all of his life, they were eviscerated by the touch of that hand. That tender hand had wreaked such havoc, the ruins of which would litter his world forever. In time, he would, he suspected, forgive that hand for being enough, for being what he wanted and needed more than what he thought he wanted and needed most.

It was not the love he had dreamt of, but those dreams had been smeared with the romances light and dark that had been hurled at him all of his life. No . . . there were no thunderclaps here, all you other fools. Just the rain that fell and washed and warmed him. There was little ardor about them. A lot of play. Sighs, yes; but few tears. No bombs . . .

Like the jazz man once said . . . "No bombs . . ."

When Jessie was young, he laid in bed and thought of dying, of what he would feel the moment before he slipped into that darkness. And now, having come close, having watched others cross the line, the thought had changed within him. Where it had been an oddity, like the notion of life on the stars, it now seemed an outrage. His Gods and his Ghosts, who in their good time and mad way answered most of his questions, if only with a smirk, had nothing for him here. On this they stood mute and stubborn. Sadistic jesters. He marched there alone, and now, with James by his side, loving James like a song, its melody more poignant, its horns thorny and wild, its whole like air, he couldn't follow any further. He just couldn't. He knew it was The Way and that none had been excused thus far, but he would have to decline. He knew he would be accused, once more, of being contrary for the sake of it, cynical, an iconoclast, weird, but no, really, taking no stands and making no statements, he just couldn't. So goodbye. May you, all of you, each and every one of you, find peace and joy there, wherever it is that you may go, wherever the end of your days takes you. Me . . . I've fought too hard for this. I've paid too high a price.

I'm not coming.

And we're lost
Out here
In the stars

OLD WOMAN

Late at night, Jessie heard the scraping of the walker against the floor. It sounded as if she dragged furniture across the room; quite an image—eighty-three-year-old Sadie in a decorating frenzy, hauling an oak china chest from one end of the dining room to the other. She had lived in this house for fifty years, since the late '30s. She heard a World War on the radio here. Here, she bore a child. She heard the language spoken shift from English to Spanish; the freeways clog with cars. Her daughter married here and bore a son nearby. She grew older here and older, and older than she ever dreamt of being. Her husband died here, and then she learned age and loneliness, all here, all in this house.

She told no one, but since the strokes, her hearing had grown worse. She feared she had suffered more. Strokes. If she told them, they'd just take her to the hospital where she would lay, idle, not even the TV to keep her company, not able to putter around like she could in her own house, putting things in order, her current task, cleaning from the closets and the cupboards the years of accumulated junk, and recalling what it all once meant to her. She did this without sentiment. Though there were personal things, some lovely things, at this point they felt hollow, as if someone had taken all the real things and left stage props in their place. Was she that far gone? Had half of her already left this world?

Her new tenant, James, had moved into the upstairs part of the house. He'd been sanding the hardwood floors. Her husband had painted them years ago and now her tenant wanted them wood again. When she was young, only poor people walked on bare wood, now the young people yearned to do so. She couldn't hear the sander, but when her cat hit the ceiling, she knew it had begun. The floor trembled beneath her. She imagined James and his friends, white-smocked, gloved, pushing huge machines like earth movers, clouds of sawdust swirling in the air like brown blizzard snow. The place was changing. They were already stripping this and painting that and making it their own. This slight trembling made her think of surgical transformations all around her, all around her lame, deaf, terribly old self. It felt as if they'd dig a hole big enough for all the house and simply slide it in with her inside, and she would die, not moving, not knowing, sitting here with her walker beside her.

James asleep beside him, Jessie heard Sadie's walker scrape across the floor. He'd only seen her from a distance, through a screen, a kind-faced, white-haired old girl sitting in a chair with the TV blaring in front of her. When she was in the hospital, he entered her part of the house when James fed her cat. The toilet had a brace attached for her to hold onto, as did the tub. The rugs were frayed, and the furniture worn. He expected the place to smell of decay, that old person smell that Mabel's house in New Orleans had. But it didn't. This place only bore the weight of time, like a tired mule from a heavy rider. It seemed anxious to slough off that burden.

The scraping of the walker stopped, signalling Sadie was back in her bed. Would this be her last night? She was ready to die. She had said as much.

"She really looked adorable," James said of his last visit with Sadie, the night before she closed her eyes and simply lost eighty-three years of treasures and pain. "She had just gotten out of bed and that wispy hair of hers was all flat on one side. She was wearing these old tennis shoes and one of her feet wasn't even in them. She was stepping on the back of it, clumping around with that walker, and she had a wedgie, her butt trying to eat that flower print shift she always wears."

Jessie liked that. Death wasn't some grim-faced specter in hooded blacks with a scythe. Death was a Warner cartoon. It gooses you and gives you wedgies, probably plants fake dog shit and speaks with a lisp. The secret, he supposed, was to make one's life as ridiculous as one's end was bound to be.

Jessie closed his eyes and felt his butt touch James'. A crunching snore rose from James' throat.

Jessie farted.

"No bombs . . ." said the jazz bandleader to his drummer—about a world in frenetic 6/8 time . . . about everything, about love and loss and probably to riff and bullshit on nothing at all, as black folks are wont to do.

"No bombs," he said. "Just . . . *'tiddy-boom.'*"

. . . Just 'tiddy-boom'

tiddy-boom.